The PLAYER

Nicola Marsh

Copyright © Nicola Marsh 2020
Published by Parlance Press 2024

All the characters, names, places and incidents in this book have no existence outside the imagination of the author and have no relation whatsoever to anyone bearing the same name or names and are used fictitiously. They're not distantly inspired by any individual known or unknown to the author and all the incidents in the book are pure invention. Any resemblance to actual events, locales, or persons, living or dead, is coincidental.

All rights reserved including the right of reproduction in any form. The text or any part of the publication may not be reproduced or transmitted in any form without the written permission of the publisher.

The author acknowledges the copyrighted or trademarked status and trademark owners of the word marks mentioned in this work of fiction.

First Published by Harlequin Enterprises in 2010 as WHAT THE PAPARAZZI DIDN'T SEE
World English Rights Copyright © 2024 Nicola Marsh

For the groupies who've wasted too much time trailing after sportsmen wishing they were WAGs. We've all been there!

Her famous smile hides a secret...

Liza Lithgow has it all—or so it seems. As a high-profile ex-WAG, she's used to the glitz and glamour of being in the spotlight. But behind the dazzling smile and designer outfits lies a woman fiercely protective of her vulnerable sister, Cindy.

A night of unexpected passion leaves Liza torn between her desires and her duties when she discovers her one night stand is Wade Urquart, the publisher who wants her tell-all story.

What starts as a simple business proposition quickly becomes complicated, because as Wade delves deeper into Liza's past, he unearths secrets that could shatter her carefully constructed world.

Desperate to protect Cindy from the fallout, Liza finds herself in an impossible situation.

Follow her head or her heart?

Chapter One

If Liza had to attend one more freaking party, she'd go insane.

Her curves resisted the constriction of the shape wear, her feet pinched from the requisite stilettos, and her face ached from the perpetual fake smile.

The *joys* of being a WAG.

Technically, ex-WAG, and loving the *ex* bit.

The reported glamorous lives of sportsmen's Wives And Girlfriends were grossly exaggerated. She should know. She'd lived the lie for longer than she cared to admit.

'One more photo, Liza?' A photographer yelled and she inwardly groaned.

That's what they all said. Not that she had anything against the paparazzi per se, but their idea of one last photo op usually conflicted with hers.

Assuming her game face, the one she'd used to great effect over the years, she glanced over her shoulder and smiled.

A plethora of flashes blinded her but her smile didn't slip. She turned slowly, giving them time to snap her side profile before she cocked a hip, placed a hand on it, and revealed an expanse of leg guaranteed to land her in the gossip columns tomorrow.

Hopefully for the last time. Being a WAG had suited her purposes but she was done. Let some other poor sap take her place, primping for the cameras, grinning inanely, starving herself so she wouldn't be labelled pregnant by the media.

With a final wave at the photographers she strutted into the function room, pausing to grab a champagne from a passing waiter, before making a beeline for her usual spot at any function: front and centre.

If this was her last hurrah, she was determined to go out in style.

She waited for the A-listers and hangers-on to flock, steeling her nerve to face the inevitable inquisition: who was she dating, where was she vacationing, when would she grant the tell-all the publishers had been hounding her for?

Her answer to the last question hadn't changed in twelve months: 'When hell freezes over.'

It had been a year since international soccer sensation Henri Jaillet had dumped her in spectacular orchestrated fashion, and three years since basketball superstar Jimmy Ro had broken her heart.

Reportedly.

The truth? She'd known Jimmy since high school and they were the quintessential golden couple: king and queen of the graduation dance who morphed into media darlings once he hit the big time. He'd launched her as a WAG and she'd lapped it up, happy to accept endorsements of clothes, shoes, and jewellery.

For Cindy.

Always for Cindy.

The PLAYER

Everything she did was for her younger sister, which was why a tell-all was not on the cards.

She'd grown apart from Jimmy and when reports of his philandering continued to dog her, she'd quit the relationship because he wanted out.

The media had a field day, making her out to be a saint, a very patient saint, and the jobs had flooded in. From modelling gigs to hosting charity events, she became Melbourne's latest 'it' girl. And when her star had waned, she'd agreed to be Henri's arm candy for a specified time in exchange for a cash sum that had paid Cindy's carer bills for a year.

Being tagged a *serial WAG* had stung, as people who didn't know her labelled her money-hungry and a camera-whore.

She tried not to care. The only people that mattered—her and Cindy—knew the truth, and it would stay that way, despite the ludicrous sums of money being dangled in front of her for a juicy autobiography.

The truth was, her life was far from juicy. She'd faked it for the cameras and readers would be distinctly disappointed to learn of her penchant for flannel PJs, hot chocolate, and a tatty patchwork quilt.

As opposed to the rumoured lack of sleepwear, martinis before bed, and thousand-thread sheets she slept on.

She had no idea why the paparazzi made up stuff like that but people lapped it up, and judged her because of it.

What would they think if they knew the truth?

That she loved spending a Saturday night curled up on the couch with Cindy under the old patchwork quilt their mum had made—and one of the few things Louisa had left behind when she'd abandoned them—watching the teen flicks her sister adored.

That she'd prefer to spend time with her disabled sister than any of the able-bodied men she'd dated?

That every word and every smile at events like this were part of a carefully constructed, elaborate mask to ensure her popularity led to continued work that would set up Cindy's care for life?

Being a WAG meant she could spend most of her time caring for Cindy; a part-time gig as opposed to a full-time job that would take her away from her sister.

It suited their lifestyle, Liza putting in infrequent appearances at galas or launches or openings in exchange for days spent attending Cindy's physiotherapy and occupational therapy sessions, ensuring the spasticity in Cindy's contracted muscles didn't debilitate her limited mobility completely.

She'd sat through Cindy's Botox injections into specific muscles to ease the pain and stiffness and deformity around joints, followed by extensive splinting to maintain movement.

She'd supported Cindy through intrathecal baclofen therapy, where a pump had been inserted into her sister's abdomen to deliver doses of the muscle relaxer into her spinal fluid to ease the spasticity and relieve muscle spasms in her legs.

She'd been there for every session of speech therapy, muscle lengthening and strengthening, splinting, orthotics, mobility training and activities of daily living management.

Putting on a façade for the cameras might've been a pain in the ass but it had been a small price to pay for the time she'd been able to spend supporting Cindy every step of the way.

The financial security her fake life provided was an added bonus.

The PLAYER

Cindy's care didn't come cheap and if a magazine wanted to pay her to put in an appearance at some B-list function, who was she to refuse?

She almost had enough money saved... After tonight she could hang up her sparkly stilettos, leave her WAG reputation behind, and start working at a worthwhile job. Something in promotions maybe, where she could put her marketing degree to use.

Cindy had progressed incredibly well over the years and Liza could now pursue full-time work in the knowledge she'd given one hundred percent with her sister's therapy when it counted.

Cerebral palsy might be an incurable lifelong condition but, with Cindy's determination, her amazing sis had reached a stage in her management plan where the spasticity affecting the left side of her body was under control and she maintained a certain amount of independence.

Liza couldn't be prouder and could now spend more hours away from Cindy pursuing some of her own goals. Though she wondered how many interviews '*serial WAG*' would garner from her sketchy CV.

A local TV host laid a hand on her arm and she faked a smile, gushing over his recent award win, inwardly counting down the minutes until she could escape.

Think of the appearance money, she mentally recited, while nodding and agreeing in all the right places.

Another thirty minutes and she could leave her old life behind.

She could hardly wait.

Chapter Two

Wade couldn't take his eyes off the dazzling blonde.

She stood in the middle of the room, her shimmery bronze dress reflecting light onto the rapt faces of the guys crowding her.

With every fake smile she bestowed upon her subjects, he gritted his teeth.

She was exactly the type of woman he despised.

Too harsh? Try the type of woman he didn't trust. The same type of woman as Babs, his stepmother, who at this very minute was making the rounds of the room, doing what she did best: schmoozing.

His father Quentin had been dead less than six months and Babs had ditched the black for dazzling emerald.

Guess Wade should respect her for not pretending. As she had for every moment of her ten-year marriage to his father.

A marriage that had driven the family business into the ground, and an irreversible wedge between him and his dad. A wedge that had resulted in the truth being kept from Wade on all fronts, both personally and professionally.

He'd never forgive her for it.

Though deep down he knew who should shoulder the blame for the estrangement with his dad.

He looked at that guy in the mirror every morning.

Wade needed to make amends, needed to ease the guilt that wouldn't quit, and ensuring his dad's business didn't go bankrupt would be a step in the right direction.

Qu Publishing currently stood on the brink of disaster and it was up to him to save it. One book at a time.

If he could ever get a meeting with that WAG every publishing house in Melbourne was clamouring to sign up to a revealing biography, he might have a chance.

Her name escaped him and, being overseas for the best part of a decade, he had no idea what this woman even looked like. He needed to do some much needed research, pronto, on the home-grown darling Australia couldn't get enough of. He'd been assured by his team that a book by this woman would be a guaranteed best-seller—just what the business needed.

But the woman wouldn't return his assistant's international calls and emails. Not that it mattered. He knew her type. Now he'd landed in Melbourne he'd take over the pursuit, demand a face-to-face meeting, up the ante financially, and she'd be begging to sign on the dotted line.

At times like this he wished his father had moved with the times and published genre fiction. It would've made Wade's life a lot easier, signing the next debut author with a commercial hit.

But biographies were *Qu Publishing*'s signature, a powerhouse in the industry.

Until Babs entered the picture, resulting in Quentin's

business sense fleeing alongside his common sense, and his father had hidden the disastrous truth.

Wade hated that his dad hadn't trusted him.

He hated the knowledge that he'd caused the rift more.

It was why he was here, doing anything and everything to save his father's legacy.

He owed him.

Wade should've been there for his dad when he was alive. He hadn't been and it was time to make amends.

The bronzed blonde laughed, a surprisingly soft, happy sound at odds with the tension emanating from her like a warning beacon. Even at this distance he could see her rigid back, and the defensive way she half turned away from the guys vying for her attention.

Interesting. Maybe she was nothing like Babs after all, who was currently engaged in conversation with a seventy-year-old mining magnate who had as many billions as chins.

Yeah, some people never changed.

Something he could do with, a change. He needed to escape the expectations of a hundred workers who couldn't afford to lose their jobs. Needed to forget how his father had landed his business in this predicament and focus on the future. Needed to sign that WAG to solve his problems. And there were many; so many problems that the more he thought about it, the more his head pounded.

What he needed most right now? A bar, a bourbon, and a blonde.

Startled by his latter wish, he gazed at her again and his groin tightened in appreciation.

She might not be his type but for a wild, wistful second he wished she could be.

Ten years of setting up his own publishing business in London had sapped him, sucking every last ounce of energy as he worked his butt off. When he initially started he'd wanted a company to rival his father's but had chosen to focus on the e-book and audio market rather than mass market paperbacks, trade, and hardbacks. Considering how dire things were with *Qu Publishing*, his company now surpassed the one-time powerhouse of the book industry.

He rarely dated, and socialised less. Building a booming digital publishing business had been his number one priority. Ironic, that he was now here to save the business he could've been in competition with if his dad had ever moved into the twenty-first century. And if Quentin had entrusted him with the truth.

Not that saving *Qu* mattered if Babs had her way.

The muscles in his neck spasmed with tension and he spun away, needing air before he did something he'd regret, like marching over to step-mommy dearest and strangling her.

He grabbed a whisky from a passing waiter and downed half of it, hoping to eradicate the bitterness clogging his throat, before making his way to the terrace that wrapped across the front of the function room in wrought-iron splendour.

Melbourne might not have the historical architecture of London but the city's beautiful hotels like this one could hold their own around the world.

He paced the marble pavers in a vain attempt to quell the urge to march back into that packed function room and blast Babs in front of everyone, media be damned.

Wouldn't that go down a treat in tomorrow's papers?

PUBLISHING CEO BAILS UP SOCIALITE STEPMOTHER, A REAL PAGE-TURNER.

He wouldn't do it, of course, commit corporate suicide. *Qu Publishing* meant too much to him.

Correction, his dad had meant everything to him and Wade would do whatever it took, including spending however long in Melbourne to stop Babs selling his legacy.

Qu Publishing needed a saviour. He intended to walk on water to do it.

He cursed and downed the rest of his whisky, knowing he should head back inside and make nice with the publishing crowd.

'Whatever's biting your butt, that won't help.'

Startled, he glanced to his right, where the bronze-clad blonde rested her forearms on the balcony, staring at him with amusement in her eyes. Blue. With tiny flecks of green and gold highlighted by the shimmery dress. A slinky, provocative dress that accentuated her assets.

The whisky he'd downed burned his gut. His excuse for the twisty tension tying it into knots.

Her voice surprised him as much as her guileless expression. Women who dressed like that usually wore calculating expressions to match their deliberate sexy garb and spoke with fake deference. She sounded...amused. Concerned. *Normal.*

It threw him.

He prided himself on being a good judge of character. Hadn't he picked Babs for a gold-digger the moment his dad introduced her ten years ago?

His people radar had served him well in business too, but something about this woman made him feel off-kilter. A feeling he wouldn't tolerate. He needed to stay focused to ensure he didn't lose the one thing that meant anything to him these days.

And as long as this woman was staring at him with that

beguiling mix of fascination and curiosity, he couldn't concentrate on anything.

'Can't a guy have a drink in peace without being accused of drowning his sorrows?'

He sounded abrupt and uptight and rude. Good. She would raise her perfect pert nose in the air and stride inside on those impossibly high heels that glittered with enough sparkle to match her dress.

To his surprise she laughed, a soft, sexy sound that made his fingers curl around the glass as she held up her hands in a back-off gesture.

'Hey, no accusations here. I was merely making an observation.'

A host of smart-ass retorts sprang to his lips and he planned on using them, until he glimpsed something that made him pause.

She was nervous.

He saw it in the way her fingertips drummed delicately on the stem of the champagne flute she clutched. Saw it in her quick look-away when he held her gaze a fraction too long. And that contradiction—her siren vamp appearance contrasting with her uncertainty—was incredibly fascinating and he found himself nodding instead.

'You're right. I was trying to take my mind off stuff.'

The corners of her mouth curved upward, the groove in her right cheek hinting at an adorable dimple.

'Stuff?'

'Trust me, you don't want to know.'

'I used to worry about stuff once.'

Intrigued by the weariness in her voice, he said, 'Not any longer?'

'Not after today,' she said, hiding the rest of what she was about to say behind her raised glass as she took a sip.

'What happened today?'

Her wistful sigh hit him where he least expected it. Somewhere in the vicinity of his heart.

'Today I secured a future for someone very important to me.'

He didn't understand her grimness or defensive posture, but he could relate to her relief. When he secured the future of *Qu Publishing* in memory of all of his dad's hard work, he'd be relieved too.

'Good for you.'

'Thanks.' She smiled again, sweet and genuine, and he couldn't fathom the bizarre urge to linger, chat, and get to know her.

She wasn't in his plans for this evening. Then again, what did he have to look forward to? Putting on a front for a bunch of back-slapping phoneys and gritting his teeth to stop from calling his stepmother a few unsavoury names?

He knew what he'd rather be doing.

And he was looking straight at her.

'Do you want to get out of here?'

Her eyes widened in surprise before a disapproving frown slashed between them. 'You've got to be kidding me. I make polite small talk for thirty-seconds and you're propositioning me?'

She shook her head, her disgust palpable.

'Let me rephrase that.' He tried his best smile, the one he used to win friends and influence colleagues. Her frown deepened. 'What I meant was, I've had a long day. My flight landed in Melbourne this morning, then I had to attend this shindig for work tonight, and I'm already tired of the schmoozing.'

He gestured at the balcony around them. 'Considering

you're out here to get away from the crowd, I assumed you're probably over it too?'

Her wary nod encouraged him to continue when he should cut his losses and run.

'The way I see it, we have two choices. Head back in there and bore ourselves silly for the next hour or we can head down to the bar in the lobby, have a martini, and unwind before we head home. I mean, before we go our separate ways.'

The corners of her mouth twitched at his correction.

'What do you say? Take pity on a guy and put him out of his misery by saving him from another interminable stint in there?'

Damn, he'd made a fool of himself, blathering like an idiot. What was it about this cool, classy blonde that had him rattled?

He'd had her pegged wrong and he, better than anyone, should know never to judge the proverbial book by its cover.

'So you weren't propositioning me?'

Was that a hint of disappointment?

Mentally chastising himself for wishful thinking, he mimicked her frown. 'Sadly, no. I'm too jet-lagged to—'

He bit off the rest of what he was about to say when her eyebrow arched.

Yep, he was screwing this up royally.

'To what?'

At last, she smiled and it made him feel oddly excited, as if he wanted to see her do it again.

'To muster up enough charm to ensure you couldn't say no.'

She chuckled and he joined in.

'I like a guy with confidence.' She laid her champagne glass on the ledge. 'Let's go get that martini.'

He didn't have to be asked twice. 'You really made me work for that acceptance.'

As he gestured for her to take the stairs ahead of him, she cast him a coy glance from beneath her lashes. 'Didn't you know? You need to work your ass off for anything worth having.'

'Is that right?'

'Absolutely.' She nodded, strands of artfully curled golden silk falling around her face in gorgeous disarray. 'Nothing better than nailing a challenge.'

He bit the inside of his cheek to prevent from laughing out loud, finding her utterly beguiling. In contrast to her sexy persona, she was forthright and rather innocent if she hadn't picked up on that nailing remark.

Then he made the mistake of glancing at her and saw the moment her faux pas registered. She winced and a faint pink stained her cheeks, making him want to ravish her on the spot.

'That didn't sound good,' she said, wrinkling her nose.

'Now we're even,' he said, wondering what they'd say after a few drinks under their belts. 'My mistaken proposition, your nailing suggestion.'

'Guess we are.' She eyed him speculatively, as if not sure what he'd say next.

That made two of them.

'Maybe we should stick to coffee tonight?'

'Why's that?'

That dimple flashed adoringly again. 'Because with our strike rate, who knows what will happen if we have a martini or two?'

He laughed. 'I was thinking the same thing.'

'Coffees it is.' She nodded, expecting him to agree.

But there was a part of him that delighted in flustering

this woman and he couldn't help but wonder how she'd loosen up with a few drinks inside her.

He leaned in close, expecting her to retreat a little, his admiration increasing—along with his libido—when she didn't.

'Actually, I prefer to live on the edge tonight. Why don't we have a martini or two and see what other verbal gaffs we can make?'

'As long as we stop at the verbal stuff,' she said so softly he barely heard her.

'Any other mistakes we make? Not our fault.'

'Oh?'

He loved her imperious eyebrow quirk.

'Haven't you heard?' He lowered his voice. 'What happens in the martini bar stays in the martini bar?'

With a surprisingly wicked twinkle in her eye, she nodded. 'That's if we stay in the bar.'

With that, she descended the steps, leaving him trailing after her, more than a little captivated by this woman of contrasts.

A woman whose name he didn't know.

With a little luck he'd have all night to discover it.

Chapter Three

Liza couldn't remember the last time she'd been out on a date.

One that hadn't been orchestrated as some huge PR stunt, that was. She'd attended media, music, and football galas on the arms of a TV personality, a rock star, and an up-and-coming footballer respectively. On each occasion, she'd been bored witless within the first ten minutes.

So what was it about this guy that had her laughing, screwing up her words, and interested in spending some one-on-one time with him?

She'd made her required appearance at the book launch. She should head home, get out of this flashy dress she'd been begged to wear by a new designer, and curl up with her e-reader and the latest juicy romance.

Instead, she watched *him* place their martini orders, shocked she didn't know his name, thrilled she didn't particularly care.

She never had fun or did anything on a whim. Ever.

Her life for the last ten years since her mum absconded

when Liza was eighteen, leaving nine-year-old Cindy in her care, had been about weighing decisions carefully to see how they would affect her younger sister.

Everything revolved around Cindy, and while Liza never begrudged her sis anything, knowing tonight would be the last time she'd have to put on her *fake face* had lifted a weight from her shoulders.

Liza could be herself from now on and Mr Martini had been in the right place at the right time. More than that, he'd intrigued her, and she couldn't say that about many men.

She'd watched him morph from uptight and judgemental to cool and a little goofy, with a hint of underlying sexiness that made her long-neglected hormones sit up and howl.

When was the last time she had sex? Probably not since Jimmy, because while Henri had paid for her arm-candy status for a year, she wouldn't go *that* far as part of their deal.

And if she couldn't remember the last time, it meant it had probably been during the good period with Jimmy, which hadn't been the last year of their relationship. The year he'd progressively withdrawn, establishing emotional distance before the final break.

Her mum had done the same over the years. In both cases, their abandonment hadn't come as any great surprise but had hurt all the same.

But tonight wasn't the time to dwell on her issues.

Tonight was perfect for something else entirely.

She did a quick mental calculation. Could it really have been four years since she'd been with a guy? Maybe that explained her irrational urge to push the limits with Mr Martini. He'd be ideal for a celebratory fling, a little fun on a night when she felt like dancing down Swanston Street with her arms in the air.

Not that she'd had a one-night stand before, but the way she was feeling right now—edgy, dangerous, a little outrageous—it could very well be a first tonight.

He stalked toward her, his ebony suit highlighting lean legs, broad shoulders, impressive chest, and she squirmed a little.

What would it be like to explore beneath that suit? To feel the warmth of a man's skin next to hers? To lose herself in the heat of passion? To assuage the yearning to experience pleasure?

Cindy was her world and Liza never regretted assuming responsibility for full-time care, but it was at times like this she wished for something she'd never have: a guy to come home to, a guy to warm her bed, a guy who wouldn't abandon her when the going got tough.

'You must really have a hankering for a martini,' he said, taking a seat next to her, far too close as a few synapses zinged with the need to touch him.

'Why?'

'Because you have an odd look on your face, like you want it real bad.'

Uh-oh. He could see her desperation? Not good.

'I'm thirsty,' she blurted, wishing the waitress would hurry up and deliver their damn drinks so she wouldn't have to stare into his knowing dark eyes.

'And I'm curious,' he said.

That made two of them. She was curious as to why she'd agreed to this and why the hell she wanted him to help celebrate her freedom tonight.

'How could two intelligent people like us, about to having a scintillating conversation, still be strangers?'

'I can rectify that.' She stuck out her hand. 'Liza Lithgow.'

'Wade Urquart. Pleased to meet you.'

As his palm touched hers and his fingers curled around her hand, Liza could've sworn every sane reason why she shouldn't indulge in a night of incredible sex with this guy melted away.

'Your name sounds familiar.' He released her hand after lingering too long. She wasn't complaining.

'I'm hoping the next words out of your mouth aren't, "Haven't we met some place before?"'

He laughed. 'No need for glib lines. You're here, aren't you?'

'True.'

And with the dim lighting, the smooth jazz spilling softly from discreet speakers, and a gorgeous guy eyeing her speculatively, she was right where she wanted to be.

For tonight only. Tonight, she was in the mood for celebrating, because finally being able to shed her old life felt amazing.

'Why did you agree to have a drink with me?' The waitress deposited their drinks and he raised a martini glass in her direction. 'You seemed to be in your element at that party.'

'Haven't you ever faked it?' She clinked her glass to his. 'What you see isn't always what you get.'

He stared at her over the rim of his glass, a slight groove between his brows. 'I must say, you're an intriguing woman and I can't figure you out.'

'What's to figure out? We're two people who wanted to escape that party and now we're having a drink, end of story.'

'Is it?'

His gaze locked on hers, potent and smouldering, and her breath hitched.

She took a sip of her martini, needing the alcohol to loosen her tightened vocal cords. 'You're expecting an epilogue?'

'A guy can always live in hope,' he said, downing his martini and placing the glass on the table in front of them. 'Honestly? I've had a crappy six months, my dad's business is under threat, and I haven't met anyone as captivating as you in a long time. So excuse me if I don't BS you.'

Liza valued honesty. Most people didn't know the meaning of the word. How many times had friends who'd hung around under the misguidance she'd take them places because of her lifestyle vanished when they learned she had a disabled sister? The stupid morons acted as if cerebral palsy were catchy, and they didn't hang around to be educated either.

Even Jimmy had been awkward and stilted around Cindy, despite Liza explaining cerebral palsy was a physical disability caused by injury to the brain before birth. Cindy had a milder form, with only the left side of her body affected by the debilitating spasticity that left her hand, elbow, hip, and knee clawed, and some speech problems. She had been lucky in escaping ataxic—or uncontrolled—movements, and athetosis, the writhing movements.

Sure, the spasticity in Cindy's elbow, wrist, and fingers made daily tasks like eating, dressing, writing, and manipulating objects difficult, but they'd learned to cope best they could. Countless occupational therapy sessions had seen to that, and the ongoing physiotherapy to prevent deforming contractures made Liza eternally grateful for the job she'd had for the last few years.

After tonight, not anymore.

Having Wade clearly articulate what he wanted impressed her. Scared the hell out of her, but definitely impressed.

'Want to talk about the crappy six months or the business?'

'Hell no,' he said, loosening the knot on his tie and unbuttoning the top button of his shirt to reveal a hint of deliciously tempting tanned skin. 'The only reason I'm in Melbourne is to sort all that stuff out, but considering I arrived this morning it can wait until tomorrow.'

'Then why show up at the party at all?'

'Because sometimes we have to do things we don't want to.'

His frown reappeared and she had a feeling he did a lot of that. He'd been frowning when she'd first seen him on the balcony, deep in thought and incredibly serious. It was what had made her approach him.

Because she used to look like that all the time when she didn't have her game face on, the one she donned along with her makeup before a public appearance. She'd frowned a lot over the years, worrying about Cindy. About her care long term should anything happen to her, about her sister's health, about her financial security.

The latter had driven her to go to great lengths. Heck, she'd tolerated posing as Henri Jaillet's girlfriend for twelve months when most people couldn't stand to be in the egotistical soccer star's presence for longer than a few minutes.

But those days were over. She'd invested wisely over the years, and tomorrow, when her investment matured, financial security would give her the peace of mind she needed to get more carer help, leaving her more time to sort out her own future.

Why wait until tomorrow?

The thought wasn't exactly out of left field. She wouldn't be sitting here if she hadn't already contemplated celebrating her newfound freedom tonight.

But how did this work? She couldn't take Wade home; she'd never expose Cindy to that unless the guy meant something to her. Even Jimmy had hardly visited and she'd known him since high school.

Though that had been more due to Jimmy's unease around Cindy than not wanting to see her. She hadn't pushed the issue with him, content to protect Cindy from any vibes she might pick up from Jimmy. But it had hurt, deep down, that her boyfriend wasn't more open-minded and didn't care enough about her to accept Cindy as part of the package while they dated.

'Another drink?'

She shook her head. 'No thanks. After the champers I had upstairs, any more alcohol and who knows what I'll do?'

'In that case, maybe I should insist you try every martini mixer on the menu?'

She smiled, glad his frown had disappeared, but a little intimidated by his stare, a probing stare that hinted there was intention behind his teasing quips.

'You could try, but you'd have to carry me out of here.'

'Not a problem. I have a suite upstairs.' He winked. 'You could recover up there.'

Guess that answered Liza's question about how she could instigate *celebrating* with Wade.

The old Liza would've laughed off his flirtation and changed the subject. The new Liza who wanted to kick up her heels for the first time in forever. Surely she couldn't pass up an opportunity like this?

'Is that an invitation or a proposition?'

'Both,' he said, capturing her hand between his, the

unexpected contact sending a buzz shooting up her arm. 'Am I in the habit of picking up women I barely know at parties? No. Do I invite them back to my place? Rarely.'

He raised her hand to his lips and brushed a soft kiss across her knuckles, making her yearn for more.

'Am I hoping you'll say yes to spending the night with me? Absolutely.'

Liza had a decision to make.

Do the sensible thing, the responsible thing, as she'd done for many years.

Or celebrate her new life, starting now.

'Do I accept offers to spend the night from guys? No.' She squeezed his hand. 'Have I had a one-night stand before? Never.' She slid her hand out of his. 'Do I want to spend tonight with you?'

She took a steadying breath and laid her hand on his thigh. 'Absolutely.'

Chapter Four

As Liza stared at the lights of Melbourne glittering below, she had second thoughts about her decision.

Was she really in Wade's suite, about to indulge in her first one-night stand at the ripe old age of twenty-eight?

She still had time to bolt. She'd thought it rather cute when he'd mentioned making a quick trip to the convenience store across the road, and it reinforced his assertion that he wasn't in the habit of picking up women or expecting to have sex his first night in Melbourne.

But while he was buying condoms, she was mulling over reasons why this might not be such a good idea after all.

She maintained strict independence for a reason. Depending on anyone for anything inevitably led to heartache.

Not that she'd be depending on Wade for anything, but letting her guard down came with a price. It left her vulnerable to *feeling* and having her defences weakened, even for a short time, made her skittish.

She'd loved her dad. He'd abandoned her without a backward glance.

She'd depended on her mum. She'd eventually left too.

She'd thought sweet, easy-going Jimmy would always be there for her. He'd done a runner too.

No, it was easier maintaining aloofness, not letting anyone get too close. And that's exactly what Wade would be doing shortly...getting exceptionally close.

Ironic, it wasn't the prospect of some stranger seeing her naked that had her half as anxious as the thought of being intimate with him and enjoying it too much.

She'd never been a needy female and had tried to instil the same independence into Cindy despite her physical limitations, yet there was something about how much she wanted to be close to Wade tonight that terrified her.

She could blame it on her impulsive need to celebrate and do something completely out of character. Or she could admit the truth, albeit to herself. That she craved a connection, even if only physical, for just one night.

The soft swoosh of the key-card in the lock had her fingers clenching the window sill.

So much for escaping.

Wade entered and her stomach dropped in an uncharacteristic swoop that signalled she really wanted this guy. She tingled all over from it, her nerve endings prickling and putting her body on notice, a heightened awareness that made her want to rub against him, skin to skin.

She'd never been so attracted to any guy before. Not even Jimmy, whose body she'd known in intimate detail from the time they'd lost their virginity together in the back seat of his car at seventeen.

Because of the clothes she wore and the persona she presented to the world, guys assumed she was an easy mark.

Even while she'd been dating Jimmy and Henri—albeit platonically in his case—guys had hit on her. Fellow soccer and basketball stars that assumed WAGs were up for anything. Commentators, managers, and agents who thought WAGs would do anything for stardom and recognition, including accept outlandish proposals.

The whole scene had sickened her and, while she'd seen enough hookups at parties in her time, she'd never been remotely interested.

What made Wade Urquart so special that she wanted to rip her clothes off the moment his sizzling-hot gaze connected with hers?

'Glad you're still here.'

He closed the door and slid off his jacket, and she caught sight of a telltale box bulging from the inside pocket. What looked like a surprisingly large box for what she'd envisioned as a brief interlude.

Her skin tingled again.

'I contemplated making a run for it.'

'What stopped you?'

He stalked towards her, stopped less than two feet away.

'This.' She laid a hand on his chest, felt the heat from his skin brand her through the expensive cotton of his shirt.

He didn't move as her palm slid upward. Slowly. Leisurely, as she savoured the contours of hard muscle, desperate to feel his skin.

He watched her, his gaze smouldering as her fingertips traced around his nipples, his breathing quickening as her fingers skated across his pecs, along his collarbone and higher. When her hand reached his neck, she stepped closer, bringing their bodies less than an inch apart.

The PLAYER

She could feel his heat. She could smell his expensive citrus aftershave. She could hear his ragged breathing.

She'd never wanted anything as badly as she wanted Wade at that moment.

With a boldness she had no idea she possessed, she tugged his head down toward her and kissed him.

The moment their lips touched Liza forgot her doubts, forgot her past, forgot her own damn name. She couldn't think beyond their frantic hands and loud moans. Couldn't get enough of his long, deep, skilled kisses.

Her body ignited in a fireball of passion and she clung to him, eagerly taking the initiative, pushing him down on the bed so he lay sprawled beneath her like a fallen angel.

His lips curved into a wicked grin as she shimmied out of her dress.

Another first. Letting a guy see her naked with the lights on.

She didn't like being seen during intimate moments. She spent enough of her life in the spotlight, being scrutinised and evaluated, she didn't need it in the bedroom too.

But this was a new Liza, a new life.

Time to shed her old habits and take what she wanted.

Starting with the sexy guy beckoning her with a crook of his finger.

'Bronze is your colour,' he said, propping on his elbows when she straddled him.

'I like to colour coordinate my outfit and underwear.'

'While I appreciate the effort—' he snagged a bra strap and tugged it down, trailing a fingertip across her collarbone and doing the same on the other side '—I'd prefer to see you naked.'

He surged upward so fast she almost toppled off, but he

wrapped his strong arms around her waist, anchoring her, holding her deliciously close. 'Now.'

She cupped his face between her hands and stared into his beautiful brown eyes. Eyes that held shadows lurking behind desire. Eyes that intrigued.

She briefly wondered if they were doing the right thing, before ignoring the doubt. She wanted to celebrate her new life tonight. Having an exciting, impulsive fling with a hot guy who made her pulse race with the barest touch was the way to do it.

She inched toward him and murmured against his mouth, 'What are you waiting for?'

Chapter Five

Wade knew Liza had vanished when he woke.

It didn't surprise him. He'd half expected her to disappear when he'd gone condom shopping.

Even now, after hours of sensational sex and a much-needed two hours' sleep, he couldn't quite believe she'd stayed.

He'd known the moment they'd started flirting she wasn't the type to deliberately reel a guy in with the intention of a one-night stand. She hadn't toyed with her hair or used fake coy smiles or accidentally on purpose touched him as so many women who came onto him did.

She hadn't pumped up his ego or been impressed by his trappings. How many times had women made a comment about his expensive watch, thinking he'd be flattered? Hell, even Babs couldn't go past a thirty-thousand-dollar watch without making some remark.

How wrong he'd been about Liza.

He'd likened her to his stepmother when he'd first seen

her surrounded by lackeys at that party. The two women couldn't be more different.

Thoughts of Babs had him glancing at his watch and leaping out of bed. He had a board meeting scheduled for ten this morning. A meeting he couldn't miss. The future of *Qu Publishing* depended on it.

While one-night stands weren't his usual style, Wade knew better than to search for a note or a business card or a scrawled phone number on the hotel notepad. But that was exactly what he found himself doing as he glanced around the room, hoping for some snippet that indicated Liza wouldn't mind seeing him again.

He might not be in the market for a relationship but his time in Melbourne would be tension-filled enough without adding frustration to his woes.

He'd been lucky enough to meet an intriguing woman who made his body harden despite the marathon session they'd had. Why not stay in touch, date, whatever, while he was in town?

He might not know how long that would be, or how long it would take to ensure the publishing business that had been in his family for centuries was saved, but having someone like Liza to distract him from the corporate stress would be a bonus.

A quick reconnaissance yielded nothing. No contact details. Disappointment pierced his hope. By her eagerness and wanton responses he'd assumed she'd had a good time too. And if she wasn't the one-night-stand type, why didn't she leave *something*? A note? A number?

Ironic, for a guy who didn't trust easily, he'd pinned his hopes on a virtual stranger trusting him enough to leave her contact details.

Then again, she'd trusted him with her body. A stupid

thought, considering he wasn't naïve enough to assume sensational sex equated with anything beyond the heat of the moment.

A glance at the alarm clock beside the bed had him frowning and making a beeline for the bathroom.

He had a boardroom to convince.

Time enough later to use his considerable resources to discover the luscious Liza's contact details.

Chapter Six

In all the years Shar, Cindy's caregiver, had stayed over, Liza had never needed to sneak past her 'the morning after'.

By Shar's raised eyebrows and smug smile as Liza eased off her sandals and tiptoed across the kitchen, only to be caught doing the walk of shame when Shar stepped out of the pantry, the time for sneaking was long past.

Liza had been sprung.

'Good morning.' Shar held up a coffee plunger in one hand, a tin of Earl Grey in the other. 'Which would you prefer?'

'Actually, I think I'll hit the shower—'

'Your usual, then.' Shar grabbed Liza's favourite mug and measured leaves into a teapot. 'Nothing like a cuppa to lubricate the vocal cords first thing in the morning.'

'My vocal cords are fine.'

Liza cleared her throat anyway, knowing the huskiness came from too much moaning over the hours that Wade had pleasured her. Repeatedly.

Shar grinned. 'Good. Then you can tell me who put that blush in your cheeks.'

Liza darted a quick glance at Cindy's door.

'She's fine. Still asleep.'

One of the many things Liza loved about Shar, Cindy being the carer's priority. Liza had seen it instantly when she'd interviewed Shar for the job after her mum had left.

Liza had been a hapless eighteen-year-old, used to looking out for her younger sister but shocked to find herself a full-time carer overnight. She'd needed help and the cerebral palsy association had come through for her in a big way. They'd organised respite care, homeschooling, assisted with ongoing physiotherapy and occupational therapy, and sent part-time carers to help.

Liza had known Shar was the best when Cindy took an instant liking to her and the older woman didn't patronise either of them.

At the time Liza hadn't needed a mother—she'd had one and look how that had turned out—she'd needed a friend, and Shar had been all that and more over the years.

Liza couldn't have attended functions and cultivated her WAG image without Shar's help and they'd eased into a workable schedule over the years. Liza spent all day with Cindy and Shar came in several evenings a week, more if Liza's WAG duties had demanded it.

Liza had been lucky, being able to devote so much time to Cindy and support them financially. And when her longterm investment matured today, she'd be sure to give Shar a massive wage increase for her dedication, loyalty, and friendship. She'd also increase Shar's hours to include days so Liza could find a job in marketing. One that didn't involve marketing herself in front of the cameras.

'Sit.' Shar pointed at the kitchen table covered in Cindy's scrapbooking. 'Start talking.'

'Damn, you're bossy,' Liza said, not surprised to find a few muscles twanging as she slid onto the wooden chair.

She hadn't had a workout like that in...forever. Though labelling what she'd done with Wade a workout seemed rather crass and casual. The passion they'd shared—the caresses, the strokes, the exploration of each other's bodies—she'd never been so uninhibited, so curious.

She knew the transient nature of their encounter had a lot to do with her wanton playfulness—easy to be bold with a guy she'd never see again.

So why did the thought leave her cold?

On waking in his bed, she'd spent an inordinate amount of time studying his features. The proud, straight nose with a tiny bump near the bridge, the dark stubble peppering his cheeks, the tiny scar near his right temple, the sensuous lips.

Those lips and what they'd done to her...oh boy.

'On second thoughts, I need more than a caffeine shot to hear this story.' Shar stood on tiptoe and grabbed the tin box storing their emergency brownie stash.

While Shar prepared the tea and chocolate fix, Liza wondered if she'd done the right thing in bolting. She had no clue about morning-after etiquette. Should she have left a thank-you note?

When she'd slid out of bed and done her best not to wake him, she'd dressed in record time yet spent another ten minutes dithering over a note. She'd even picked up a pen, only to let it fall from her fingers when she'd stared at the blank hotel paper with fear gripping her heart.

As she'd looked at that paper, she'd been tempted to leave her number, before reality had set in. Wade hadn't questioned her about her life or made polite small talk. He hadn't been interested in anything beyond the obvious—her body—and that was enough of a wake-up call for her to grab her bag and get the hell out of that hotel room.

One-night stands were called that for a reason. That was all they were. One night. The uncharacteristic yearning to see him again? To have a repeat performance of how incredible he made her feel?

Not happening.

'Right, here we go.' Shar placed a steaming cup of Earl Grey tea in front of her along with two double-choc-fudge brownies on a side plate. 'Get that into you, then start talking.'

Liza cupped her hands around the hot cup and lifted it to her lips, inhaling the fragrant bergamot steam. Earl Grey was her comfort drink, guaranteed to make her relax.

She'd drunk two pots of it the morning she'd woken to find her mum gone. It hadn't been a shock. Louisa had been an emotionally absent mother for years before she'd left. Guess Liza should be grateful her mum had waited until Liza turned eighteen before she'd done a runner, leaving her the legal guardian of Cindy.

Crazy thing was, Liza had long forgiven her father for running out on them after Cindy's birth. Some men were fickle and couldn't stand a little hardship. She'd come home from school to find her dad shoving belongings into his car in front of her stoic mum. Louisa had cried silent tears, holding a twelve-month-old Cindy in her arms, while her dad had picked Liza up, hugged her tight, and told her to take good care of her sister.

She'd been doing it ever since.

While Liza might have forgiven—and forgotten—her dad, she couldn't forgive her mum as easily. Louisa had watched Cindy grow. Had been a good mum in her own way. But Liza had seen the signs. The subtle withdrawing of affection, longer respite visits away from the girls, the scrimping and saving of every cent.

Her mum hadn't left a note either. She'd just walked out of the door one morning with her suitcases and never looked back.

If Louisa expected Liza to be grateful for the birthday cards stacked with hundred-dollar bills that arrived every year on Cindy's birthday, she could think again.

Cindy needed love and caring, not guilt money.

Thankfully, with what Liza had done over the last decade, Cindy's financial future was secure and they no longer needed her mum's money. Now Liza needed to start doing stuff for *her* and first item on the agenda involved finding her dream job. One that didn't involve schmoozing or showing her best angle to the cameras.

She sipped at the tea, savouring the warmth.

'Could you drink any slower?' Shar wiped brownie crumbs off her fingers and mimicked talking with her hand.

Liza placed a cup on the saucer and reached for a brownie, and Shar slapped her wrist. 'You can eat later. I want details, girlie.'

Liza chuckled. 'I better tell you something before you break a bone.'

Shar's hand continued to open and shut, miming chatter. 'Still not enough of this.'

'Okay, okay.' Liza leaned back and sighed. 'Henri's book launch was every bit as boring and pompous as him. I was doing the rounds, talking to the regular people. I got bored as usual.'

Then she stepped out onto that balcony and her life changed in an instant. Melodramatic? Hell yeah, but no matter where her future led, she'd never forget that one incredible night with Wade.

'And?' Shar leaned forward and rubbed her hands together.

'I needed some fresh air, so I headed outside, and met someone.'

'Now you're talking.'

Liza sighed. How to articulate the rest without sounding like a floozy?

'Shar, you know Cindy is my world, right?'

Shar's eyes lost their playful sparkle and she nodded, sombre. 'I've never seen anyone as dedicated as you.'

'Everything I've done is for my little sis and I'd do it again in a heartbeat, but last night signalled a new beginning for me and when the opportunity to celebrate presented itself? Well, let's just say I grabbed it with both hands.'

Shar let out a soft whoop and glanced at Cindy's door. 'Good for you.' She leaned forward and wiggled her eyebrows. 'So how was he?'

Liza made a zipping motion across her lips. 'No kissing and telling here.'

Shar reached across and patted her forearm. 'All I can say is, about time, love. You're a good girl, dating those dweebs to secure your financial future, making the most of your assets. About time you had a little fun.'

'There was nothing little about it,' Liza deadpanned, joining in Shar's laughter a second later.

'Hey, Liza, is it chocolate cereal time?'

Liza's heart squished as it always did at the sound of Cindy's voice from behind her bedroom door.

There was nothing she wouldn't do for her sister.

'You know the drill. Muesli as usual,' Liza called out,

draining the rest of her tea before heading to the bedroom to help Cindy dress.

'Are you going to see him again?' Shar asked, as Liza paused with her hand on the doorknob.

Liza shook her head, the disappointment in Shar's expression matching hers.

Silly, as Liza didn't have time for disappointments. She had a secure investment about to mature, a new career in marketing to embark on, and an easier life ahead. No time at all to reminisce about the hottest night of her life and what might have been if she'd had the courage to leave her details.

'Trade you a pancake stack for the muesli,' Cindy said, as Liza eased open the bedroom door.

The moment she saw Cindy's beaming, lopsided smile, Liza wiped memories of Wade and focused on the number one person in her life and her sole motivation.

Life was good.

She didn't have room in it for commanding, sexy guys, no matter how unforgettable.

Chapter Seven

With Cindy engrossed online, Liza ducked into the shower, something she should've done the moment she arrived home to scrub off the lingering smell of Wade's aftershave.

Maybe that was why she hadn't? Because the moment she towelled off, slipped on her skinny jeans and a turquoise long-sleeved T, and padded into the kitchen to say bye to Shar, she missed his evocative crisp citrus scent.

Irrational? Absolutely, but it wasn't every day an amazingly hot guy left his designer aftershave imprinted on her skin.

The perky hum died in her throat as she caught sight of Shar waving a stack of messages at her.

'These are for you.'

Liza raised an eyebrow. 'All of them?'

Shar nodded. 'I didn't want to bombard you when you first came in.'

'More like you wanted the gossip and knew those would distract me.'

'That, too.' Shar grinned and handed them over. 'Looks like some editor from *Qu Publishing* is mighty persistent.'

Liza groaned. 'Can't those morons get a life and stop badgering me?'

'Doesn't look like it.' Shar pointed to the message slips in her hand. 'All those are from her.'

'No way.'

Liza flicked through the lot, twelve in all. Nine yesterday when she'd been out in the afternoon and later at the party, three while she'd been in the shower this morning.

'She said she'd call back in ten minutes.'

'Like hell.' Liza stomped over to the trash and dumped the lot. 'I'm sick to death of being pestered by this mob and I'm going to put a stop to it.'

Shar punched the air. 'You go, girl.'

Liza grinned. 'While I'm kicking some publisher butt, maybe you should stop watching daytime reality TV?'

'Cheeky.' Shar shooed her away. 'You've got an hour before I need to leave, so hop to it.'

Liza didn't need to be told twice.

No way, no how, would she ever sell her story. Cindy needed to be protected at all costs and the last thing Liza wanted was a bunch of strangers reading about their lives and intruding.

They would, she had no doubt. There would be book tours and blog tours and a social media explosion if she revealed everything about her life to date. It was why these *Qu Publishing* vultures were hounding her. They knew a bestseller when they saw it.

Laughable, really, because what would they say if they knew the truth, that she'd invented a fake life to protect her real one? That every event, every lash extension, every designer gown, had fitted a deliberate persona she'd cultivated to get what she wanted.

Lifelong security for her little sister.

And when her financial adviser called today and gave her the good news about her investments maturing, she could put away her lash curler and hair straightener forever.

Yeah, the sooner she set this publisher straight, the better.

She yanked on black knee-high boots and shrugged into a sable leather vest with fake fur collar. While being a WAG had been a pain, some of the perks, like the gorgeous designer clothes she got to keep on occasion, had been great.

She'd miss the clothes. She wouldn't miss the rest.

Time to hang up her stilettos and set the record straight.

* * *

Wade strode into the boardroom with five minutes to spare, then spent the next thirty listening to a bunch of boring agenda items that could've been wrapped up in half that time.

He wished they'd cut to the chase. The future of *Qu Publishing* depended on a bunch of old fuddy-duddy's that wouldn't know a profit margin if it jumped up and bit them on the ass. The members of the board were old school, had been best buddies with his dad and, in turn, were *'rather fond of his delightful wife Babs.'*

When the chairman had articulated that little gem at the party last night, Wade wanted to hurl. Was he the only guy who could see through her fake wiles?

By the board's decision to back Babs in her quest to sell *Qu Publishing*? Hell yeah.

He knew it would take a monumental effort to save this

company. From the accounts down to the staff, *Qu* needed a major overhaul. And to do that they needed a cash injection, in the form of a mega bestseller.

Which reminded him, he needed to sign that WAG to a contract today. He'd up the ante with a massive cash injection from his own pocket, a hefty six-figure sum she couldn't refuse. From what he'd heard in snippets from memos, her sordid tale would be a blockbuster. Serial WAG dated an international soccer star and a basketball player, a media darling from magazines to TV, a practised socialite who'd appeared everywhere in Australia from all reports.

He couldn't care less if she'd dated the entire soccer team and what she'd worn to do it, but that kind of gossip drivel made the average reader drool. And sold books.

Thankfully, his company had branched out into the lucrative young adult market and were making a killing, but *Qu* readers expected factual biographies so no use getting too radical when he'd probably only have a few months tops to save the company.

Yeah, he needed to get that WAG to sign ASAP. He'd get straight onto it, once this meeting wound up.

'And now, gentlemen, we come to the last item on the agenda.' The chairman cleared his throat and glared at Wade as if he'd proposed they collectively run down Bourke Street naked. 'As you've seen from the proposal Mr Urquart *Junior* emailed us yesterday, he wants to give the company three months to see if it can turn a healthy profit.'

Wade bristled at the emphasis on junior. He'd paid his dues in this company in his younger days, and had done a hell of a lot more in London where his business was booming compared to this languishing one.

Thoughts of the disparity saddened him and pricked his guilt as nothing else could. If he hadn't been so pig-headed, so stubborn, so distrustful, he could've helped his dad while he had the chance. Could've done a lot more too, such as mend the gap between them that *he'd* created. A regret he'd have to live with for the rest of his life. A regret that would be appeased once he saved *Qu*.

'To do this, he proposes *Qu Publishing* will have a *New York Times* bestseller on its hands within the year, along with an accompanying publicity blitz in the form of social media, television, and print ads.'

A titter of unease echoed around the conference table and Wade squared his shoulders, ready for the battle of his life. No way would he let Babs win. She'd made a laughing stock out of his dad; damned if he sat back and let her do the same to his dad's legacy.

'We usually put agenda items like this to a vote.' The chairman steepled his fingers and rested his elbows on the table like a presiding judge. 'But I don't think it's necessary in this case.'

Wade clenched his hands under the table. Pompous old fools. 'Gentlemen, if you'd let me reiterate my proposal—'

'That won't be necessary, Wade.'

The chairman's use of his first name surprised, but not as much as his dour expression easing into a smile. 'Every member here knew your father and respected what he achieved with this company. But times are tough in the publishing industry. The digital boom has hit our print runs hard and readers aren't buying paperbacks or hardbacks like they used to. Economically, it makes sense to sell.'

Wade opened his mouth to respond and the chairman held up his hand. 'But we admire what you've achieved with your company in London. And we like your ambition. It reminds us of your father. So we're willing to give you three months to turn this company around.'

Jubilant and relieved, Wade nodded. 'Thanks for the opportunity.'

'We understand the profits won't soar until we have that promised bestseller on our hands, but if you can prove to us we'll have that guaranteed hit with buyers' pre-orders in three months, we won't vote with Babs to sell *Qu*. Got it?'

'Loud and clear.' Wade stood, ready to hit the ground running.

His first task? Get that WAG to sign on the dotted line. 'Thanks, gentlemen, you won't be sorry.'

He'd make sure of it.

Chapter Eight

The idiots were stonewalling her and Liza wasn't happy.

'You won't take no for an answer. Your editors won't take no for an answer, so I'm taking this to the top.' She leaned over the receptionist, who, to her credit, didn't flinch. 'Who's your boss?'

The receptionist darted a frantic glance to her right. 'He can't see you now.'

'Like hell.' Liza strode towards the sole double doors where the receptionist had looked.

'You can't do that,' the perky blonde yelled and Liza held up her hand.

'Watch me.'

Liza didn't stop to knock, twisting the door knob and flinging open the door before she could second-guess the wisdom of barging into a CEO's inner sanctum unannounced.

This publishing company were relentlessly harassing her; let them see how they liked getting a taste of their own medicine.

The editors wouldn't listen, so the only way she'd get this mob to leave her alone was to have the order given from the top.

However, as she strode into the office, her plan to clear up this mess hit a major snag.

Because the guy sitting behind a huge glass-topped desk, the guy barking orders into a phone, the guy clearly in charge of *Qu Publishing*, was the guy who'd set her body alight last night.

* * *

Wade stopped mid-sentence as Liza barged into his office like an avenging biker chick—tight denim, clingy long-sleeved T-shirt, black leather vest, and the sexiest knee-high boots he'd ever seen—her expression grim and her eyes blazing.

Wow.

He'd expected to never see her again, yet secretly hoped he would. But he'd never thought she'd end up in his office the morning after their unforgettable night.

After the crappy year he'd endured—learning his dad hadn't trusted him with the truth about his heart condition, accepting how far their relationship had deteriorated, his dad's death, Babs' sell-out plans—maybe the big guy upstairs had finally granted him a break.

'Set up a meeting with the buyers and we'll discuss covers and digital launch later,' he said, hanging up on his deputy without waiting for an answer.

He stood, surprised by Liza's stunned expression. It wasn't as if they were strangers. She'd obviously sought him out, though the dramatic entrance was a surprise. He'd been told most people couldn't get past Jodi, the receptionist. His dad had raved about her and from what Wade had seen of her work ethic in half a day, the woman was a dynamo.

Maybe Liza had been so desperate to see him she couldn't wait?

Yeah, and maybe that WAG would saunter into his office any second and give him her completed biography bound in hardcover.

'Hey, Liza, good to see you again—'

'*You're* the CEO of *Qu Publishing*?'

She made it sound as if he ran an illegal gambling den, her eyes narrowing as she crossed his office to stand on the opposite side of his desk. 'It makes sense now. That's why you slept with me.'

She muttered an expletive and shook her head, leaving him increasingly clueless as he waved away Jodi, who'd stuck her head around the door, and motioned for her to close it. Jodi mouthed an apology before doing as he said, leaving him alone with an irate, irrational woman who stared at him as if she wanted to drive a letter opener through his heart.

He wished he'd stashed it in his top drawer once he'd opened the mail.

'Time out.' He made a T sign with his hands and gestured toward the grey leather sofas. 'Why don't we sit and discuss this?'

Whatever *this* was, because he had no idea why she'd gone crazy at him for being CEO of *Qu* and what that had to do with having great sex.

Her lips compressed in a mutinous line as she marched toward the sofas and slumped into one, ensuring she sprawled across it so he had no chance of sitting nearby.

Ironic, when last night she couldn't get close enough, and the feeling had been entirely mutual.

Even now, with confusion clogging his head, he couldn't switch off the erotic images. Liza straddling him. Underneath him. On her hands and knees in front of him. The sweet taste of her. The sexy sounds she made. The softness of her skin. The intoxicating rose and vanilla scent that had lingered on his sheets.

Their night together had been sensational, the most memorable sex he'd had in a long time.

Hell, he was hard just thinking about it.

Then he looked into her dark blue eyes and saw something that shocked him.

Betrayal.

What had he done to make her look at him as if he'd ripped her world apart?

'You used me,' she said, jabbing a finger in his direction before curling it into a fist as if she wanted to slug him. 'Proud of yourself?'

'I don't know what you're talking about.' He poured a glass of water and edged it across the table. 'Can we backtrack a little so I have a hope in Hades of following this bizarre conversation?'

'Drop the innocent act. The moment I walked in here and saw you, everything made sense.'

Her fingers dug into the leather, as if she needed an anchor. 'Why you asked me to have a drink with you last night, inviting me back to your suite, the sex...' She trailed off and glanced away, her blush rather cute. 'I can't believe you'd stoop that low.'

She thought he'd used her. Why? None of this made sense.

'From what I remember, you approached me on that

balcony. And from your participation in the phenomenal sex, you were just as into it as me.'

Her blush deepened as she dragged her defiant gaze to meet his. 'What I don't get is why you'd think I'd sell my story after I discovered your identity?'

She shook her head. 'Or are you so full of yourself you thought I'd remember the sex and sign on the dotted line?'

Pieces of the puzzle shifted, jiggled, and finally aligned in a picture that blew his mind.

'*You're* the WAG we're trying to sign?'

'Like you didn't know.' She snorted in disgust. 'Nice touch last night, by the way. "*Your name sounds familiar?*" Shit. I can't believe I fell for it.'

Hot damn.

Liza Lithgow was the WAG he needed to save *Qu Publishing*.

And he'd slept with her.

Way to go with messing up big time.

'Liza, listen to me—'

'Why the hell should I?' Her chest heaved with indignation and he struggled to avert his eyes. No use fuelling her anger. 'You *lied* to me. You *used* me—'

'Stop right there.' He held up his hand and, amazingly, her tirade ceased. 'Yeah, I knew *Qu Publishing* was pursuing a WAG for a biography but I had no idea that was you.'

'But I told you my name—'

'Which I had vaguely heard but, come on, I'd only landed in Melbourne for the first time in six months a few hours earlier and came into the office briefly before heading to that party. So yeah, I'd probably seen your name on a document or memo or something, that's how it registered.'

He leaned closer, hating how she leaned back. 'But

everything that happened between us last night? Nothing to do with us publishing your biography and everything to do with...'

Damn, it wouldn't do any good blurting out what last night had been about. He didn't need her feeling sorry for him. He needed her onside, ready to tell her story so the board gave *Qu* more than a temporary reprieve.

'With what?'

At least her tone had lost some of its vitriol.

'With you and me and the connection we shared.'

'Connections can be manufactured,' she said, her steely stare speaking volumes.

She didn't believe him.

When he'd first glimpsed her last night, he'd associated feminine and bimbo in the same sentence. Then when she'd spoken to him, he'd re-evaluated the bimbo part pretty damn quick. He never would've thought her attractive outer shell hid balls of steel.

'Maybe, but the way we burned up the sheets last night?' He smiled, trying to charm his way out of this godforsaken mess. 'I wasn't faking it. Were you?'

At last, a glimmer of softening as her shoulders relaxed and her glare lost some of its warrior fierceness. 'Forget last night—'

'Big ask,' he said, continuing with his plan to use a little honey rather than vinegar to coerce her into giving him a fair hearing. 'I don't know about you, but the way we were together last night? Pretty damn rare.'

She glanced away, but not before he glimpsed a spark of heat in those expressive blue eyes.

'And I have to say, I was pretty disappointed this morning to find you gone, because I would've really liked to...'

The PLAYER

What? See her again? Pick up where they'd left off? Prove their attraction extended beyond a first-time fluke?

Best he stop there.

He needed this woman onside to save his father's business. A business he should've seen was floundering before it was too late. Before his prejudices had irrevocably damaged his relationship with his dad and ended with him not knowing his dad was dying before he could make amends.

Saving *Qu*, his dad's legacy, was the one thing he could do to make this semi-right. He could live with the guilt. He couldn't live with knowing he hadn't given this mission his best shot.

Her gaze swung back, locking on his with unerring precision. 'I'll admit we shared something special last night. But I don't have room in my life for complications.'

He should drop this topic and move on to more important stuff, like getting her to sign. But he couldn't help tease her a little. Maybe if she loosened up he'd have more chance of convincing her *Qu Publishing* were the only mob in town worth considering for her tell-all tale?

'And you're saying I'd be a complication if I called you for a date? Dinner? A movie?'

She nodded. 'You're a nice guy but—'

'Nice?' He winced. 'Ouch.'

She rolled her eyes. 'Your ego's not that fragile, considering you picked me up at a party after knowing me less than ten minutes.'

'And you're not as immune to me as you're pretending considering you agreed to a drink after knowing me less than ten minutes.'

'Touché.' The corners of her mouth curved upward. 'Let's forget last night and move on to more important matters, like why your office is bugging me constantly and won't take no for an answer.'

'Glad to hear the editors are doing their jobs.'

Her mouth hardened. Maybe he'd taken the levity a tad far?

'You think this is a joke?' She shook her head, her ponytail swishing temptingly over one shoulder, reminding him of how her blonde hair had looked spread out on the pillows and draped across his chest. And lower.

'I can't count the number of phone calls to my cell, and now someone in your office has used underhanded tactics to discover my *unlisted* landline number and I'm being pestered at home? Poor form.'

She sighed and a sliver of remorse pierced his resolve to get this deal done today.

'I hate having my private life invaded and it's time you and your cohorts backed off.'

He should feel guilty but he didn't. While Liza didn't fit the typical WAG profile, she couldn't live the life of a famous sportsman's girlfriend without loving some of the attention. Having her private life open to scrutiny came with the territory.

All he wanted was to delve a little deeper, give his readers something more, and they in turn would give him what he needed most: money to save *Qu*.

'What if we don't back off?'

He threw it out there, expecting her to curse and threaten. He wasn't prepared for the shimmer of tears that disappeared so fast after a few blinks he wondered if he'd imagined them.

'Two words for you.' She held up two fingers. 'Harassment charges.'

The PLAYER

Idle threats didn't scare him. But the guilty twist his heart gave at the sight of those tears absolutely terrified. He didn't handle waterworks well. Even Babs' crocodile tears at his dad's funeral had made him supremely uncomfortable.

That had to be the reason he'd gone soft for a moment and actually considered backing down after seeing Liza's tears.

'Maybe if you gave us a chance to explain our offer, you may feel differently?'

Her expression turned mutinous. 'There's nothing you can say or do that will persuade me to sell my story.'

He was done playing it cool. He'd tried the truth; she hadn't believed him. He'd tried charming her; she'd lightened up for a scant minute. Time to go for the jugular, and do his damnedest to forget that his lips had coaxed and nipped her in that very vicinity last night.

'A ghost writer, a mid-six-figure advance, a more than generous royalty percentage, all for a story that most people have probably heard before?'

Her glacial glare dropped the temperature in the room by five degrees. 'It's called *private* life for a reason. I don't give a flying fig what people surmise or print or think about me. As of last night, I'm done with all the hoopla, so you and your cronies can invent a fictional story for all I care.'

The first flicker of unease soon gave way to fear. Wade never took no for an answer in the business world. But Liza's adamant stance put a serious dent in his confidence he could woo her to Qu.

He needed her biography.

Failure wasn't an option.

'Look, Liza, I'm sure we can come to some type of mutually beneficial agreement—'

'What part of *you can take your offer and stick it* don't you understand?'

With that, he watched his final chance of saving his father's legacy stride out of the door.

Chapter Nine

Liza made it to the elevator when her phone rang. Considering her hands shook with fury she wouldn't have answered it if she hadn't been expecting her financial adviser's call imparting good news.

Her portfolio of investments had matured and Cindy was set for life. The figures she'd crunched for longterm ongoing medical and allied health care had terrified her, but now, after years of careful saving and investing, she could rest easy in the knowledge should anything happen to her Cindy would be financially secure.

It made every blister from impossibly high stilettos, every sacrificed chocolate mousse so not to gain weight, every artful fend-off from a groping sleaze, worth it.

Ignoring the death glare from the receptionist, she fished out her phone, checked the number on display, and hit the answer button.

'Hey, Walden, good to hear from you. I've been expecting your call.'

A long silence greeted her.

'Walden?'

A throat cleared. 'Uh, sorry, Miss Lithgow, this is Ullric.'

Okay, so Walden's assistant had called instead. A first, but not surprising considering Walden had a full schedule whenever she'd tried to slot in a meeting lately.

'Hey, Ullric. I'm assuming you have good news for me about my investments?'

Again, a long pause, and this time a finger of foreboding strummed Liza's spine.

'About that...' His hesitancy made her clench the phone. 'I'm afraid I have some bad news.'

Liza's heart stalled before kick starting with a painful wallop. 'I don't like the sound of that. What's happened?'

Ullric blew out a long breath that transferred into annoying static. 'Mr Wren has disappeared and his clients' funds are gone.'

Liza's legs collapsed and she sagged against the nearest wall.

This couldn't be happening.

It had to be a delusion brought on by the shock of discovering Wade had potentially used her.

Though she wasn't prone to delusions, and Ullric's pronouncement underlined with regret seemed all too real.

'What—how—?'

'The fraud squad is investigating. His assets have been seized, but from what I've been told the client funds have been siphoned into offshore accounts.'

Liza swore. Several times. The only words she could form let alone articulate.

'I'm sorry, Miss Lithgow. The police will be in touch and I'll let you know if I hear anything—'

Liza disconnected, the phone falling from her fingers and hitting the carpet with a muted thud.

Her life savings.

Gone.

In that moment, every stupid awards ceremony and dress fitting and magazine article she'd endured flashed before her eyes in a teasing kaleidoscope of humiliation.

Everything she'd worn, everything she'd said, for the last umpteen years, had been to build a sizeable nest egg for Cindy in case something happened to her.

And now she had nothing.

Tears burned the backs of her eyes and a lump welled in her throat.

What the hell was she going to do?

A pair of expensive loafers came into view and her head fell forward until her chin almost touched her chest. Great, that was all she needed to make her failure complete. Wade Urquart to witness it.

'I think this belongs to you.'

He picked up her phone and held it out.

Liza was bone-deep tired, exhausted to the core, where she'd regularly drawn on a well of courage to face the media, the crowds, the critics.

But she had to leave here with some snippet of dignity intact and right now, sitting in a crumpled heap on Wade's expensive carpet, she'd lost most of it.

'Here.' He dropped the phone into her open bag and held out his hand. 'Let me help you up.'

'I think you've helped enough,' she muttered, but accepted his hand all the same, grateful for the hoist up as her legs wobbled.

'Are you okay?'

She couldn't look at his face, didn't want to see the pity there, so she focused on the second button of his crisp pale blue business shirt.

He'd lost the tie, a snazzy navy striped one that had set off his suit earlier. The fact she'd noticed? A residual tell from her WAG days when it paid to be observant about the latest fashion, and nothing to do with how she could recite every item of clothing he'd worn last night and what he'd looked like without it.

When she didn't answer, he placed his hand under her elbow and guided her toward his office.

'Come with me.'

Liza wanted to protest. She wanted to yell at the injustice of busting her butt all these years and for what? But all the fight had drained out of her when she'd hung up and it wouldn't hurt to have a glass of water, muster the last of her meagre courage, and face the trip home.

Home. Where Cindy was.

Damn.

She'd had their future all figured out. Now she had nothing. She needed to find a job, and pronto. The idea of trying to juggle a new job and how it would affect Cindy's care, without the security of money... Pain gripped her chest and squeezed, hard.

The tears she'd been battling welled again and this time spilled over and trickled down her cheeks.

Wade darted a glance her way but she resolutely stared ahead and dashed away the tears with her other hand.

Thankfully, he didn't question her further until he led her to the sofa she'd so haughtily vacated five minutes earlier, and closed the door. He didn't speak, setting a glass of water in front of her and taking a seat opposite, giving her time to compose herself.

His thoughtfulness made her like him, and she didn't want to, not after what she'd discovered today. In fact, when she'd huffed out of here, she'd assumed she'd never see him again—and had steadfastly ignored that small part of her that had been disappointed at the thought.

She gulped the water, hoping it would dislodge the giant lump of sadness in her throat. It did little as she battled the hopelessness of her situation.

Her new life? In ruins.

Cindy's financial safety net? Gone.

She'd been screwed over by some smarmy financial adviser whose balls she'd crush in a vice if she ever laid eyes on him again. As if that were likely.

Her financial ruin meant she was back to square one, but no way could she don designer outfits and start prancing around on some egotistical sportsman's arm again.

Mentally, she couldn't take it any more. Physically, late twenties was getting old for a WAG and she was done with the paparazzi scrutiny.

Which left her plum out of options.

'Want to tell me what happened out there?'

'Not really.' She topped up the glass from a water pitcher, grateful her hand didn't shake.

'I don't think my offer was that repugnant so it had to be something else?'

'It was your offer.'

The lie tripped off her tongue. Better for him to think that than know the truth. That she'd lost her life savings and had no way out of this disastrous situation.

'You're not a very good liar.'

'How would you know?'

He raised an eyebrow at her acerbic tone. 'Because contrary to what you believe, I actually spent time paying attention to you last night and I reckon you've got one of the most guileless faces I've seen when you let your guard down.'

Damn, how did he do that, undermine her with insight when he shouldn't know her at all?

'I can't talk about it.' She shook her head, tugging on the end of her ponytail and twisting it around her finger. 'Besides, it's my problem. There's nothing you can do about it.'

'Sure?' He braced his elbows on his knees. 'Don't forget, if you're ever in a bind all you have to do is accept my offer and you'd be set for life.'

As his words sank in, Liza's hand stilled and she flicked her ponytail back over her shoulder.

No. She couldn't.

But what other option did she have?

Agreeing to a revealing biography would replenish her lost savings and ensure Cindy's security. Relating a few stories to a ghost writer had to be less painful than going down the fake tan/lash extensions/hair foils route again. She wanted to pursue a career in marketing and accepting this book deal would allow that.

The only catch was Cindy.

Liza didn't want the world knowing her private business and she wanted to protect Cindy at all costs. She'd done a good job of it so far, keeping her public persona completely separate from the reality of her home life.

Any publicity shots and interviews with Jimmy had been done at his palatial apartment; same with Henri. It had been important to her, deliberately misleading the press to think she lived with the sport stars so they wouldn't hound her or, worse, follow her.

Not that she was ashamed of the modest Californian bungalow she shared with Cindy, but her goal to ultimately protect Cindy at all costs meant she wanted their real home and the life they shared to be off-limits to the public.

The PLAYER

The guys had never mentioned Cindy in interviews either, though she knew that had more to do with them not wanting to be tainted—even by association—with a disability they couldn't handle or had no knowledge of rather than her request.

Jimmy and Henri were too egotistical to want to field questions about their girlfriend's disabled sister so they'd pretended Cindy hadn't existed. While their apparent disregard had hurt, it had been exactly as Liza wanted it.

Her protecting Cindy over the years had worked, but how could she sustain that in a biography? Then again, she'd invented a physical façade for years, playing up to the image of the perfect WAG.

What if she invented a story to go with it?

It wasn't as if she hadn't done it before when she'd been interviewed. She'd give a few scant details, an embellishment here, a truth stretched there. No one would be wiser if she did the same in her biography.

She could lay out the basics of her upbringing and focus on the interesting stuff, like her relationships with Jimmy and Henri. That was what people were really interested in anyway, the whole 'what's it like dating a famous sports star?' angle.

Yeah, she could do this. Continue her WAG role a little longer, but behind the scenes this time. Had to be easier than strutting in front of A-listers and faking it.

But she'd told Wade to shove his offer so appearing too eager would be a dead giveaway something was wrong and she didn't want him prying.

If she had to do this, it had to be a strictly business deal. From now on, her personal life was off-limits. Unless it involved inventing a little drama for the ghost writer.

'What if I was crazy enough to reconsider your offer? What would it entail?'

He masked his surprise quickly. 'We'd have a contract to you by this afternoon. Standard publishing contract with clearly stated royalty rates, world rights, advance, option to your next book.'

Next book? Heck, she could barely scrimmage enough suitably juicy info for this one. Though she'd love to publish a book raising the awareness of cerebral palsy and give an insight for carers. It was something she'd considered over the years: using her high profile to educate people regarding the lifelong condition.

But then she imagined the intrusiveness on Cindy's life—the interview requests, the demands, the interference on her schedule, and the potentially damaging physical effects linked to emotional fragility in those with CP—and Liza balked.

Cindy thrived on routine and the last thing Liza wanted for her sister was a potential setback. Or, worse, increased spasticity in her muscles because she got too excited or too stressed. Most days were hard enough to get through without added complications and that was what spot-lighting her sister's cerebral palsy could do.

Embellishing her so-called glamorous life and leaving Cindy out of it would be a lot easier.

'How much is the advance?'

He named a six-figure sum that made her head spin. Were people that desperate to read a bunch of stuff about her life?

Considering how she'd been occasionally stalked by paparazzi eager for a scoop while dating Jimmy and Henri, she had her answer.

'The advance is released in increments. A third on signing, a third on acceptance of the manuscript, and a third on publishing.'

'And when would that be?'

'Six months.'

She laughed. 'You're kidding? How can you publish a book in six months?'

'Buyers are lined up. A ghost writer is ready to start tomorrow if you can. Week-long interview process, two weeks writing the book, straight to copy and line editors, then printers.'

Liza knew little about publishing but marketing was her game and she'd interned at a small publishing house while at uni. No way could a book get turned around in six months. It took an average of eighteen months to get a paperback on shelves.

'Do you have a marketing plan?'

A slight frown creased his brow. 'I have to admit, *Qu* is lagging in that department at the moment. I want to bring the company into the twenty-first century with online digital instalments of books, massive social media campaigns, exclusive digital releases on our website, subscribers, that kind of thing.'

'So what's the problem? Hire someone.'

He tugged at his cuffs, the first sign she'd seen him anything but confident since she'd arrived.

'Turnaround time on this book is tight.'

'I'll say.' She shook her head. 'Six-month release date? Impossible.'

'And you can say that with your extensive publishing experience?'

She didn't like his sarcasm, didn't like the fact it hurt more.

'Matter of fact, I interned for a publisher during my marketing degree.'

'Next you'll be telling me you're applying for the job.'

And just like that, Liza had a bamboozling idea. For the first time since that soul-destroying phone call earlier, hope shimmered to life and gave her the confidence to retake control of her life.

'That's a great idea. Why don't you give me the marketing job on this book and I'll make sure it's the best damn book this company has ever published?'

He fixed her with an incredulous stare. 'Let me get this straight. You want a publishing contract *and* a marketing job here? After basically telling me to stick my offer—'

'Call it a WAG's prerogative to change her mind.' She smiled, hoping it would soften him up. 'What do you say? Do we have a deal?'

'What we have here is you not telling me everything and then having the cheek to try and coerce me into giving you a job too.'

'Take it or leave it.'

Yeah, as if she could afford to call his bluff.

If he left it, she'd be back to strapping on her stilettos and smiling for the cameras again. She shuddered.

After a few fraught seconds, the sensual lips that had explored every part of her body eased into a smile.

'You drive a hard bargain, Liza, but you've got yourself a deal.'

Liza could've hugged him. She settled for a sedate shake of hands, though there was nothing remotely sedate about the way her body buzzed as his fingers curled around hers.

The part of her plan where she kept dealings with Wade strictly business would be sorely tested.

Chapter Ten

Wade had given up trying to figure out women a long time ago.

He dated them, he wooed them, he liked them, but that's where it ended. Any guy who lost his head over a woman was asking for trouble.

He'd seen it firsthand with his dad.

Not that he'd begrudged the old man happiness, far from it. Quentin had raised him alone after his mum died when he was a toddler, devoting his time to his business and Wade with little room for anything else. When Wade started uni, Babs had come along and his dad had been smitten. Wade had been appalled.

He'd seen right through the gold-digging younger woman; probably why Babs had hated him on sight.

The feeling had been entirely mutual.

But Wade had seen the way his dad lit up around Babs and while he'd tried to broach the delicate subject of age differences and financial situations, one ferocious glare from his dad had seen him backing down.

Quentin and Babs had married within a year, and as

much as Wade hated to admit it, Babs had been good for his father. They'd had a good ten years together, but Wade left for London after two. He couldn't pretend to like Babs and vice versa, and he saw what the barely hidden animosity did to his dad. It caused an irrevocable tension between them, and while neither of them mentioned it, it was there all the same.

Wade had stayed away deliberately, only catching up with Quentin on his infrequent trips to London, invariably alone. They talked publishing and the digital revolution and cricket but Wade never asked how Babs was and his dad never volunteered the information.

He hadn't seen his dad in the fifteen months before his death and Quentin hadn't trusted him enough to tell him the truth about the heart condition that had ultimately killed him, resulting in the biggest regret of Wade's life and the sole reason he was here, trying to save the company that had meant the world to his dad.

He should've known about his dad's dodgy heart. He should've had the opportunity to make amends for deliberately fostering emotional distance between them. Instead, Quentin died and guilt mingled with sorrow for Wade, solidifying into an uncomfortable mass of self-recrimination and disgust.

He didn't trust easily and his scepticism of Babs had ultimately driven his dad away.

He regretted it every day since.

Hopefully, saving *Qu* would help ease the relentless remorse that he'd screwed up when it came to Quentin.

While Wade had left *Qu* a long time ago, he kept abreast of developments, and when rumours of employee dissatisfaction, low print runs, poor sales, and financial strife reached him in London following Quentin's death, he knew what he had to do.

Throw in the fact his dad had barely been buried before Babs started flinging around terms like 'white elephant' and 'financial drain' in relation to *Qu*, and Wade had had no choice.

He'd appointed his deputy as acting CEO in London and hightailed it back to Melbourne as fast as he could. Just in time too, judging by the board's lukewarm response to his plans to save the business.

As for his confrontation with Babs before the party yesterday...he'd been right about her all along.

Thank goodness his dad had been smart enough to leave a precise will. Babs got the multimillion-dollar Toorak mansion and a stack of cash. Wade got the business. But sadly, the bulk of his dad's shares had passed on to Babs too, and that meant they now had equal voting rights with the board of *Qu Publishing*.

If she whispered in the right ears—and she had from all accounts—and it came to a vote, they'd sell company out from under him.

He couldn't let that happen. He wouldn't, now he had Liza on board.

Thinking of Liza brought him full circle back to his original supposition.

He'd given up trying to figure women out. Which was why he had no clue why she'd had a mini meltdown half an hour earlier, and why he didn't trust her complete about-face in regard to his offer.

One minute she'd been fiery and defiant, the next he'd found her in a defeated heap near the elevator. Whoever had called had delivered bad news, and the thought it could've been some guy who'd devastated her rankled.

He'd assumed she was entanglement-free last night, but what if there was some guy in the picture, an ex she was hung up on? And why the hell did it matter?

Whatever had happened via that phone call, it had provided a major shake-up for her to switch from a vehement refusal to accepting his offer. It made him wonder, had it been a ruse? A plan on her part to get him to up the advance?

He didn't think so, because her devastation had been real when he'd found her crumpled beside the elevator. But his ingrained lack of trust couldn't be shaken and her vacillating behaviour piqued his curiosity meter.

Was Liza genuine or was she a damned good actress? And if so, what was her motivation?

Ultimately, it shouldn't matter. He couldn't afford to be distracted. It would take all his concentration to ensure her autobiography hit the shelves within a record six months. He had editors, buyers, online marketing managers, and a host of other people to clue in to the urgency of this release.

Not that he'd tell them why. Having a publisher on the brink of implosion didn't exactly inspire confidence in the buyers who'd stock this book in every brick-and-mortar and digital store in the country.

He needed their backing for Liza's story to go gangbusters following a speedy release. It would take every moment of his time to make it happen.

So why the persistent niggle that having Liza stride into his office the first time, and later agree to his offer, was the best thing to happen to him on a personal level in a long time?

He'd been thinking about contacting her anyway, doing an online search first and if that hadn't worked, getting one of the company's investigators to find her. Thankfully, that wasn't necessary. But realising she was the WAG every publisher in town had been hounding for a tell-all threw him. And made him doubt his own judgement, which he hated.

Had his first impressions been correct? Was she a woman not to be trusted?

He couldn't afford to have this book deal fall through and with Liza's abrupt turnaround—shirking his offer then accepting it—what's to say it wouldn't happen again?

She'd verbally agreed to the deal, but until he had her signature on a contract he wouldn't be instigating any processes.

Damn, he wished he knew her better so he could get a handle on her erratic behaviour. She seemed introverted last night, reluctant to flirt, at complete odds with the image of WAGs.

In London, a day didn't go by without the tabloids reporting exploits of sports stars' wives and girlfriends, from what they wore to a nightclub opening to rumours of catfights.

The woman he'd coaxed into having a drink with him last night, the woman who'd later blown his mind with sensational sex, didn't fit his image of a WAG.

Which begged the question, what had Liza done to become notorious?

What was her real story?

Considering he'd just emailed her a publishing contract, guess he'd soon find out.

Chapter Eleven

Liza had less than twenty-four hours to come up with a plausible life story.

One far removed from the truth.

She'd been in a daze on the tram ride home from the publisher's office, stunned how quickly her life had morphed from orderly to disastrous.

Though it could've been a lot worse if she didn't have Wade's offer to agree to. Because as much as it pained her to contemplate he might have used her to get what he wanted, she'd be in real trouble if his publishing contract hadn't been on the table.

It had pinged into her inbox the moment she'd arrived home and she'd scoured the contract, expecting hidden clauses and a bunch of legalese. Surprisingly, the contract was straightforward and the sizeable advance eased the constriction in her chest that had made breathing difficult since she'd taken that call from Ullric.

Once she'd forwarded it to Jimmy's manager—who also happened to be one of the best entertainment lawyers in the country—she sat down with a pen and paper, determined to have bullet points ready for her first meeting with the ghost writer tomorrow.

Wade wanted a specific kind of book: a complete tell-all highlighting the juicy, glamorous, scandalous aspects of her life as a WAG. Yet another reason why she'd have to leave Cindy out of it.

He'd also assured her the story of her life would be well written and focused on the facts, but Liza read widely and was wise enough to know ghost writers liked to embellish, taking a little fictional creativity along the way.

Let them. Considering she was doing the same thing, giving an embroidered account of her life while withholding important facts—namely Cindy's existence—she couldn't begrudge the writer that.

Why should she care? Wasn't as if the media had never invented stuff about her to sell papers or magazines. While she'd been with Jimmy there'd been a never-ending list of supposed indiscretions. Smile at a world champion tennis pro and she was accused of having an affair. Lean too close to hear a rock star's boring diatribe at a nightclub, ditto. Wear a revealing dress by a handsome new designer, she'd got it for free by sleeping with him.

She'd grown immune after a while, knowing the invented scandals were the bane of a WAG's existence but a price she had to pay. Though not a day went by when she didn't feel like telling the truth and ramming her side of the story down their lying throats.

Besides, when she'd arrive home after yet another movie premiere or restaurant opening or fashion-label launch, curl up next to Cindy on the couch and cuddle her innocent sister, Liza knew it was all worthwhile.

There was nothing she wouldn't do for her little sis, including manufacture a life story to give the masses something they'd probably invent anyway, and secure Cindy's future in the process.

* * *

Liza arrived at *Qu Publishing* at nine on the dot the next morning, dressed to impress and armed with her extensive list.

She wanted to wow the ghost writer, and to do that she'd donned her WAG persona, from sleek blown-out hair to lashings of makeup, seamed stockings and sky-high black patent leather stilettos, to a tight crimson sheath dress with long sleeves and low neckline.

Power dressing at its best and if the reaction of the guys who passed her on Collins Street was any indication, she'd achieved her first goal: make a dazzling first impression.

She found it infinitely amusing that guys would barely give her a second glance when she did the grocery shopping with her hair snagged in a low ponytail and no makeup, wearing yoga pants and a hoodie, yet dressed in a slinky outfit with enough makeup to hide a million flaws and they drooled.

Fickle fools.

As she paced the reception area she wondered if that was what had captured Wade's attention at the party, her fake outer shell. Was he a player? Or had her name been enough, and he'd wanted her to sign on the dotted line all along?

Then again, what he'd said had been true. *She'd* approached *him*. Engaged him in conversation. Even flirted a little, and he hadn't known her name. Not until later at the bar.

His admission had soothed her wounded ego for all of

two seconds before she realised a smart guy like him would've researched her to get as much info on the WAG he wanted so badly, and would've known what she looked like from the countless pictures online.

Stupid thing was, she wanted to believe him, wanted to give him the benefit of the doubt that the way they'd hooked up at the hotel had been about a strong sexual attraction and a mutual need to escape. But Liza had been let down by people her entire life, especially those closest to her, and had learned healthy distrust wasn't such a bad thing.

She'd idolised her dad. He'd left when he couldn't handle having a disabled daughter. She'd idolised her mum, yet her mother hadn't been able to handle things either. When Louisa had finally left it had almost been a relief because the tension in the house had dissipated and Liza had been more than happy to step up with Cindy.

She'd been doing it for years anyway.

While she wanted to hate Wade for using sex as a way to get her onside, part of her couldn't help but be grateful his offer had still been on the table after the way she'd stormed out of his office.

Without that contract and advance, she'd be screwed.

And he'd given her a job to boot.

Not many executives would've given in to her crazy demand for a job alongside a significant contract offer, but he'd done it. Probably out of desperation to have her agree to his proposal, but whatever his rationale, she was grateful.

He'd agreed to let her focus on marketing her biography for a start, which was a good way to ease into her new career. She might've been handed a dream job on a platter but she hadn't actually worked in marketing since she gained her degree six years earlier, so his faith in her went some way to restoring her confidence.

Thought she knew if she screwed this up, not only would she have an irate publisher on her hands, she'd be fired before her job had begun.

So for now, along with spinning a bunch of embellished half-truths for the ghost writer, she had to spend her days coming up with whiz-bang marketing plans and meeting with Wade.

She didn't know which of the three options terrified her most.

As if she'd conjured him up, Wade opened his door and strode toward her, tall and powerful and incredibly gorgeous. She'd rubbed shoulders with some of the most handsome guys in the world, from movie stars to sporting elite, but there was something about Wade Urquart that made her hormones jump-start in a big way.

He wore his dark hair a tad long for convention and sported light stubble that accentuated his strong jaw. Throw in the deep brown eyes, the hot bod, and the designer suit that highlighted his long legs and broad shoulders, and Liza wasn't surprised to find herself holding her breath.

Though the clothes didn't impress her as much as the body beneath; she'd seen every inch, touched every inch, and her skin prickled with awareness the closer he got.

'Punctual. I like that.' His slow, easy grin added to her flustered state as she shook his hand and looked like an idiot when she snatched hers away too fast.

'I'm eager to get started.' She gestured at her bag. 'I've brought a ton of notes and photos and stuff so we can hit the ground running.'

'That's what I like to hear.'

She fell into step beside him, having to lengthen her stride to keep up.

'I can't emphasise enough the speedy turnaround

needed on this.' He stopped outside a conference room and gestured her in. 'There's a lot riding on this book being a runaway success.'

A wave of panic threatened to swamp Liza, mixed with a healthy dose of guilt. Inventing a bunch of lies to protect Cindy hadn't seemed so bad when she'd been jotting notes last night, but hearing the hint of desperation in Wade's voice made her wonder about the wisdom of this.

What if one of her lies unravelled? What if she was declared a fraud? Or, worst-case scenario, what if she exposed Cindy in the process?

'Something wrong?'

Everything was wrong, but Liza had to do this. It was the only way forward that enabled her to provide a safe future for Cindy while following her own dream at the same time. She was used to depending on no one but herself, and to provide Cindy with that same independence, she had to make this work.

She faked a smile that had fooled the masses before. 'Let's get started.'

With a doubtful sideways glance, he gestured her ahead of him into the room, where he introduced her to Danni, the ghost writer, a forty-something woman who reeked of efficiency.

'I'll leave you ladies to it,' he said, glancing at his watch. 'And I'll see you in my office this afternoon at one-thirty, Liza.'

'Sure,' she said, not looking forward to the marketing meeting one bit.

She might be able to fake it for Danni, but Wade had seen her naked. Not much more she could hide from him.

Over the next four hours Liza laid bare her life. The life she'd pared back, embellished, and concocted, that was.

Danni taped their interview, jotted notes in a mega scrapbook already filled with scrawl, and typed furiously into a laptop.

Danni asked pertinent questions, nothing too personal but insightful all the same and Liza couldn't help but be impressed. And relieved. This biography business was going better than expected and, according to Danni, she'd have enough information by the end of the week to collate into a workable chapter book.

When they finally broke at one fifteen, Liza had a rumbling tummy and a headache, but she couldn't afford to be late for her meeting with Wade so she grabbed a coffee from the lunch room, checked in with Shar to see how Cindy was, and made it to Wade's office with a minute to spare.

He barely acknowledged her entrance when she knocked and he waved her in, his eyes riveted to the massive monitor screen in front of him while on a conference call. Whoever was on the other end of the line was spouting a whole lot of figures that made her head spin; hundreds of thousands of dollars bandied around as if they were discussing pocket change.

She could hardly comprehend the advance *Qu Publishing* had offered her. It topped the other offers she'd had by two hundred grand. Ironic, it hadn't been enough to tempt her when she'd had her investments maturing but, with her nest-egg gone, beggars certainly couldn't be choosers.

'Sorry about that,' he said after ending the call, clasping his hands together and resting them on the desk. 'I've been working on the pre-orders, which are all important.'

'How many people are interested in reading about my boring life?'

'Boring?' He spun the screen around and pointed at the spreadsheet covered in figures and highlighted colours. 'According to the orders flooding in already, you're ranking up there with the best for notoriety.'

He leaned back, pinning her with a speculative stare. 'Which makes me wonder, what have you done that is so newsworthy?'

Liza shrugged, knowing he would've asked this question eventually but feeling increasingly uncomfortable having to discuss any part of her life with him.

Rehashing details for Danni was one thing; baring herself—metaphorically—to Wade another.

'Not much, really. My high-school sweetheart turned out to be a soccer superstar so we were thrust into the limelight early on.'

She smoothed a fray in her stockings, remembering how out of her depth she'd felt at the time. Photographers snapping their photo wherever they went, groupies slipping phone numbers into Jimmy's pocket constantly, autograph hunters thrusting pen and paper into his face regardless of appropriate timing.

It had been a circus but she'd quickly learned to play the game when a national magazine had offered her twenty-thousand dollars for an interview. At twenty-two and fresh out of uni it had been an exorbitant sum, and she'd grabbed it to buy a new motorised wheelchair for Cindy.

That interview had been the start. More had followed, along with interviews on talk shows, hosting charity events, and appearing at openings for a fee. Jimmy had encouraged her and with every deposit in her investment account she'd been vindicated she was doing the right thing.

Cindy would be secure for life. Liza never wanted her sister to struggle the way she had when their parents had left them. Being abandoned had been bad enough, but left without long-term security? Liza could never forgive her folks for that.

Not that she heard from them. Her dad had vanished for good when he'd left and her mum occasionally called on birthdays and Christmas, along with sending those cards with a hundred dollar bill for Cindy. Liza never took her calls, letting Cindy chatter enthusiastically, while she wondered the entire time how a parent could walk out on their child.

Especially a high-needs child.

'Did you travel much?'

She shook her head. 'No, I didn't want to become one of those women who clung to their man.'

And she couldn't leave Cindy for long stints, not that Wade needed to know that. It was one of the things that had eventually come between her and Jimmy. He needed full-time glam eye candy on his arm wherever he went; she needed to devote time to her sister. They'd parted on amicable terms despite what the press said.

But her heart had been a teeny-weeny bit broken because he was the first guy she'd ever loved, the only guy she'd ever loved.

And he'd walked away, just like her folks.

Thankfully, she'd developed a pragmatic outlook to life over the years and, while Jimmy continued to be plastered over the media, she was glad she'd stepped off his bandwagon.

'I thought that's what WAGs do. Pander to the whims of their superstar partners. Hand-feed them grapes. Fan them with palm fronds. Give them facials on demand.'

He was winding her up and her lips curved in an answering grin.

'You forgot being on call twenty-four-seven.'

He snapped his fingers. 'Thanks for clarifying.'

'Actually, you're not far off the mark.'

He arched a brow and she continued. 'You're on show every time you step out. Scrutinised all the time. It felt like a full-time job in the end.'

'Is that why you broke up?'

'Something like that.'

She didn't know if he was asking these questions in a professional capacity or assuaging his curiosity, but for now she was happy to answer. Sticking to the facts was easy. It was the potential landmine questions she'd need to carefully navigate.

'And then you dated a basketball star.'

She wrinkled her nose and he laughed. 'That good, huh?'

'Off the record? Henri and I had a convenient arrangement. Nothing more.'

Confusion creased his brow. 'How did that work?'

'He needed a girlfriend. I needed the lifestyle he provided.'

She threw it out there, gauging his reaction.

His eyes widened and his lips tightened, his frown deepening.

'I don't understand.'

She shrugged, as if his opinion didn't matter, when it irked he thought badly of her. Not that it should surprise her. They hardly knew each other, despite one night of amazing sex.

But for someone who'd spent the last umpteen years being judged by everyone, it really pissed her off to add Wade to that list.

'Our fake dating arrangement was mutually beneficial. That's all anyone needs to understand.'

He recoiled as if she'd slapped him. 'I hope you'll be giving us more than that in the book.'

'My biography will be comprehensive.'

He continued to stare at her as if she'd morphed from an angel to the devil incarnate and she struggled not to squirm beneath the scrutiny. When the silence grew painfully uncomfortable, she gestured to the stack of paperwork on his desk.

'Shall we discuss the marketing plan?'

'Yeah,' he said, his frown not waning as he spread documents across his desk and picked up his pen. 'I have a few ideas but I want to hear what you've come up with.'

Chapter Twelve

As Liza ran through an impressive list of ideas, from a massive social-media blitz via popular online sites to weekly bonus e-serials exclusive for *Qu Publishing* subscribers, Wade wondered how he could have misjudged her so badly.

Maybe he could blame it on jet lag, because he could've sworn the live-wire he'd wooed into bed a couple of nights ago was far removed from the calculated, cool woman who was happy to date as part of an *arrangement*.

He'd seen a lot of interesting couples in his travels over the years, younger women in a relationship with older men for the money and security. Hell, he'd seen it firsthand with Babs and his dad.

So why did he find the thought of Liza hooking up with some slick sports star for the sake of *lifestyle* so unpalatable?

'What do you think?'

Damn, she'd caught him out.

'Sorry, I was still pondering your book tribe idea. What did you ask?'

Nice save but, by her narrowed eyes, she didn't buy it.

'With the new e-book releases of any sporting personnel three months before my biography launches, why not insert a snippet from the bio into the back of those books? Build a little anticipation?'

'Sounds great.'

She'd come up with some solid ideas and he was impressed with her work ethic. Pity he couldn't say the same about the rest.

'How do you feel about the serial WAG tag?'

She stiffened in surprise. 'That's out of left field.'

He shrugged, pretending her answer wasn't important, when he needed to know what made her tick. Because sitting across from her, the faintest rose fragrance scenting the air and reminding him of the way it had clung to his skin after their night in his suite, he had to know who the real Liza Lithgow was.

Was she the soft, hesitant woman he'd met at the party and spent a wild, passionate night with? Or was she a gold-digging, fake floozy who'd do anything to further her lifestyle?

'Call it publisher curiosity,' he said, hating how her answers meant way more to him than on a publishing level.

'I've been called many things by the press over the years, serial WAG being on the tamer side.'

Her flat monotone suggested rote answers, when he wanted to know the *real* her. It annoyed the hell out of him.

'How did you put up with all that?'

'Came with the territory,' she said, darting a nervous glance at the documentation on his desk, as if she'd much rather be discussing business than her personal life.

Too bad. He wanted to know more about the investment his dad's company was riding on and right now he had the distinct feeling she was hiding something. Something that went beyond a need for some degree of privacy.

He couldn't pinpoint what it was but her general evasiveness, the look-away glances, the rote answers, seemed too trite, too polished, almost as if she'd rehearsed.

A crazy suspicion? Maybe, but he'd put his father's company and three hundred grand of his own money on the line for this book. It had to be a blockbuster and so far Liza hadn't inspired him with her careful answers and measured responses.

'You haven't told me why every publisher in Melbourne was clamouring for your exclusive story,' he said, prepared to keep interrogating her until she told him the truth.

'Don't you know?'

'Know what?'

'I slept with the entire international Aussie soccer team,' she deadpanned. 'The English one too.'

He barked out a laugh. 'I don't believe you about the English. I would've read about that in London.'

'Pity my antics didn't make it all the way over there,' she said, her tone holding a hint of accusation. 'What is it you want me to say? That I danced naked at a grand final? That I had half a rugby team and cheerleaders in my room one night?'

Her voice had risen and she lowered it, making him feel guilty for pushing her. 'Honestly? I have no idea why my story is so important, other than the fact I haven't given them a story before now.'

She held out her hands, as if she had no tricks up her sleeves. 'I've been reticent in interviews over the years. I pick and choose the ones I do and the questions I answer. Maybe that's fostered the mystery surrounding my life? Plus I've dated two mega-famous Aussie sporting stars, and maybe people want to know, "Why her? What's so special about her?"'

He'd touched a nerve. He could see it in the frantically beating pulse in her neck, in the corded muscles, in her rigid shoulders.

He could move in for the kill now he had her more animated and far removed from her trite answers, but something in her eyes stopped him.

She looked almost haunted. As if she'd seen too much, done too much, and was still reeling from it.

It made him even more curious.

What or who had put that look in her expressive eyes?

'Want to take a break and meet back here at four-thirty?' He asked, feeling bad for pushing her hard for answers.

Liza nodded and stood before he'd barely finished the sentence, desperate to escape. Yeah, he'd definitely hit a nerve.

He watched her walk to the door, a goddess in sheer stockings, a tight red dress, and heels that could give a guy serious ideas.

'Liza?'

She glanced over her shoulder and arched a brow.

'Good work on the marketing campaign.'

'Thanks.' Her smile lit her expression and made her eyes sparkle, the first genuine show of emotion all afternoon.

Interesting. Either this book or this marketing job meant more to her than she was letting on.

'See you later,' he said, as she slipped out of the door with a wave, leaving him more bamboozled than ever.

What he really wanted to say was, *would the real Liza Lithgow please let me in?*

Chapter Thirteen

Liza surreptitiously slid the sleeve of her dress up to check her watch.

On the plus side, Wade had stopped interrogating her during their second meeting of the day and had concentrated on marketing plans.

On the downside, it was six o'clock and she was on the verge of fainting from lack of food.

Her stomach rumbled on cue and she wrapped an arm over it. Too late. His gaze zeroed in on it. The rumbles were quickly replaced by a horde of tap-dancing butterflies as she remembered the way he'd stared at her naked body on that unforgettable night.

Damn, she'd vowed not to think about that night again, especially when working. She'd done a good job of it so far, then all it took was one casual glance from him and the entire evening flashed across her mind in vivid detail.

His hungry stare as he'd propped over her, their bodies joined and writhing slowly.

His sensual lips as he'd kissed and nipped the inside of

her elbows, her thighs, her stomach, every zone more erogenous than the last.

His skilful hands as he'd brought her to orgasm. Repeatedly.

Great. The butterflies had stilled, only to be replaced by a fiery heat that had her gritting her teeth to stop from squirming.

'Hungry?'

'A little,' she said, as her stomach gave another growl akin to a muted roar.

He laughed. 'Sorry, I'm used to working through when I'm on tight deadlines.'

His eyebrows arched when he glanced at the time on his PC screen. 'Didn't know it was so late. Want to grab a bite to eat so we can keep working?'

'Sure.'

Thank goodness she'd had the foresight to ring Shar before this meeting started. With a four-thirty start she'd had a feeling it would run late.

'Have you been to *Mexie's*?' He shrugged into his jacket. 'I've heard it's a favourite in Melbourne.'

'Good choice,' she said, surprised they were going out for dinner. 'The food's sublime.'

When he'd suggested grabbing a bite to eat she'd expected ordered-in sandwiches while he kept her chained to the desk.

Chained... Like how he'd pinned her wrists overhead as he entered her the first time...

Uh-oh. She needed to stay work-focused and hope to hell he didn't pick up on her sudden shift in thoughts.

'Let's go.'

He opened the door for her and as she stepped through

with him close behind a ripple of awareness raised the hair on the back of her neck.

It disarmed her, this unexpected physical reaction when she least expected it. Several times during their meeting she'd experienced a buzz from perfectly innocuous actions, like their fingers brushing when handing over documentation or a lingering glance a tad longer than necessary.

She'd been deliberately brusque, determined not to botch this opportunity, which was exactly what would happen if she acknowledged the attraction between them now he was her boss.

Not forgetting that little technicality of him potentially using her that one incredible night despite his protestations of innocence.

No, she'd be better off forgetting their night of scintillating sex and concentrating on getting her story straight for the book and making her marketing ideas fly. She had enough complications in her life without adding fraternising with the boss to them.

They made small talk as they strolled down Flinders Lane and Liza tried to ignore the way people turned to stare. Considering they were both tall and well dressed, she could attribute it to natural curiosity. Or she could acknowledge it for what it was: once a recognised WAG, always a recognised WAG.

When would people forget whom she'd dated and move on to the next WAG? Sure, she'd milked her image for all it was worth, most recently hosting a reality show that had been a ratings disaster yet the most talked-about event on social media sites for months.

But she was done with that part of her life. Wasn't that the main reason she'd slept with Wade in the first place, celebrating putting her past behind her and moving on to a new life?

Ironic, her past had caught up with her and collided with her future.

When they arrived at the Melbourne institution, the nightly queue of eager patrons dying to try the fabulous Asian food was thankfully small, but Liza knew they'd still be ushered to the bar downstairs to wait for a table to become available.

Not good. When she'd agreed to have a meal with Wade, she hadn't envisaged the two of them sitting too close in a bar reminiscent of their first night together, and the last thing she needed right now was any reminder. Her body hummed with his proximity. Sharing a drink in a cosy setting? Trouble.

Their wait for a table wouldn't be too long according to the hostess so Liza headed downstairs with Wade, trying to ignore his hand on the small of her back and the accompanying reaction that made her knees wobble a tad.

It worsened when they took a seat at the bar and their thighs brushed. Hell, what had Liza let herself in for?

'Drink?'

'Soda with a twist of lemon,' she said, desperate to reassemble her wits and not needing alcohol to add to her bedazzlement.

'Technically we're off the clock, so you can have a drink, you know.'

'Isn't this a working dinner?'

He nodded but she didn't trust the glimmer of mischief in his eyes. 'Maybe I should order you a martini again and see what happens?'

'*That* won't be happening again,' she said, squeezing her knees together for good measure.

He laughed and nudged her with his elbow, the slightest contact making her body tingle with awareness. 'Never say never, I reckon.'

'We are *so* not going there.' She glared as if she meant business.

By his answering wink, he was thinking monkey business.

'I'll let you in on a secret,' he said, leaning so close his breath fanned her ear, pebbling her skin in the process. 'It's okay to flirt outside the office. Especially after we've already—'

'No flirting,' she said, unable to suppress a smile when he blew on her ear for good measure.

'That's better.' He touched a fingertip to the corner of her mouth. 'First time I've seen you lighten up all day.'

He traced her lower lip, lingering in the middle, and she couldn't have formulated a coherent answer if she tried.

'Don't get me wrong, I like how focused you are on helping us meet this all-important deadline, but today?' He pulled a funny face, complete with crossed eyes. 'You were seriously scary.'

'Was not,' she said, enjoying his antics despite her vow to keep things purely platonic from now on.

She liked that he could switch from mega-powerful corporate CEO to teasing. It was one of the things that had attracted her that first night, the way he lightened up when they started talking.

'Yeah, you were.' He bumped her gently with his shoulder. 'But not to worry. I've got all night to get you to loosen up.'

'All night?' She wished.

'Figure of speech.' His wicked grin implied otherwise. 'Though I have to tell you, I was blown away when you barged into my office yesterday. It was like all my prayers had been answered.'

Liza didn't want to go there. She should change the subject, fake an emergency trip to the loo, anything to quell the irrational surge of jubilation that he'd been happy to see her.

'We really shouldn't talk about that night. It's unprofessional—'

'Why did you bolt without leaving contact details?'

A host of callous retorts designed to maintain distance between them sprang to her lips, but Liza settled for the simple truth.

'Because I didn't think you wanted more than one night.'

She put the onus back on him. No way could he admit to wanting more without appearing a little needy.

'Considering we'd only just met, I don't think either of us knew what we wanted beyond the amazing connection we shared. But later...' he shrugged and turned toward the bar, but not before she'd seen a flicker of something akin to regret darken his eyes 'let's just say I was disappointed to find you gone.'

Liza admired his honesty. He sounded so genuine she could almost believe he hadn't known her identity when they slept together.

It made her curious. What would've happened if they'd had more than one night?

'For argument's sake, let's say I left my number.'

The waiter deposited their drinks and he took a sip of whiskey before turning back to face her. 'I would've called you. Asked you for a date.'

'Before or after offering me a publishing contract?'

The PLAYER

He grimaced. 'Got to admit, that does complicate matters now I know.'

There he went again, reiterating he'd had no idea of her real identity that night at the party. Maybe she should give him the benefit of the doubt?

When it came to liars, she had a pretty good radar. She could tell when someone was uncomfortable with Cindy from ten paces and hated when people acted as if cerebral palsy were contagious. It had driven a wedge between her and Jimmy, between most of her friends too. Which suited her fine, because most of them had drifted away as Jimmy became more famous and their lives changed.

It had started with her school friends pulling away, girls she'd grown up with and who she assumed she could always count on. But the more fancy events she attended with Jimmy, the faster the snide remarks started, and she found herself not invited to their parties or dinners or girls' nights out.

Being abandoned by her friends had sucked and she'd learned to cultivate light-hearted friendships with acquaintances, fellow WAGs who stuck together out of necessity. But they'd pretty much abandoned her too once she broke up with Jimmy, and later Henri, and she missed her old friendships more than ever.

True friends stuck around through life changes. Guess she didn't have any true friends.

'Hey, you drifted off for a second.' He touched her hand and a lick of heat travelled up her arm.

'It's more than a complication now I'm working for you and you know that,' she said, re-evaluating the wisdom of working for him when his simple touch made her skin sizzle.

'Co-workers have relationships all the time,' he said,

stroking the back of her hand with his thumb. 'And don't forget, the only reason you're working for me is because you blackmailed me into giving you a job.'

'Good point.' She chuckled, proud for pulling that masterstroke. 'So you're trying to get into my pants again on a technicality?'

His thumb paused and his eyes widened in surprise. 'Are you always this blunt?'

Not always. Most of her life she'd watched what she said and what she ate and what she wore, presenting a perfectly poised persona to the world, desperate no one saw behind the façade.

If she didn't let people get too close they couldn't hurt her. A motto she'd learned to live by the hard way.

So what was it about this guy that had her more relaxed than she'd ever been?

She took a sip of soda and shrugged. 'We've seen each other naked. I don't see the point in playing coy.'

He mouthed 'wow' and squeezed her hand before releasing it. 'Okay, the least I can do is return the favour. I like you. You intrigue me. So while I'm in Melbourne, I'd like for us to see each other.'

Liza hadn't seen that coming. She'd thought Wade might put the hard word on her for another night of rousing sex. No way did she expect a quasi-relationship for the time he was in town.

She was tempted. Seriously tempted. How long since she'd had great sex or indulged in genuine fun? Probably in the early Jimmy days, before the fame and the expectations associated with living up to the WAG label. She knew time spent with Wade would involve both sex and fun.

But what about Cindy and the lies she'd constructed to protect her?

The PLAYER

If she started dating Wade, how long could she keep him from visiting her place? How long before her lies unravelled and her carefully constructed story came crashing down?

She couldn't afford to have *Qu Publishing* renege on the contract, nor did she want to lose her first real marketing job.

Getting involved with Wade could compromise both.

'Wade, I like you—'

'I can sense a *but* coming.' He winced and pretended to clutch his heart. 'Give it to me straight. I'm a big boy, I can take it.'

She managed a wan smile. 'But I don't want to complicate our business arrangement.'

Disappointment downturned his mouth for a moment, before those lips she'd experienced over every inch of her body curved into a seductive smile.

'I understand. You don't know me that well. But the way *Qu Publishing* secured your book deal was by sheer persistence.' He raised his glass in her direction. 'I don't give up easily. Challenge is my middle name.'

He clinked it to hers, his stare filled with wicked promise. 'Don't say I didn't warn you.'

Chapter Fourteen

Liza had been in a quandary when Wade offered to drive her home.

She'd wanted to refuse because it had been bad enough having him charm her over a delicious dinner of green Thai chicken curry, slow-cooked garam masala beef, and exquisite peppered calamari.

But she'd wanted to get home fast so she could spend time with her Cindy before sister went to bed so she'd agreed. And was now ruing her impulsive decision as he walked her to the front door.

Politeness demanded she invite him in for a coffee.

Self-preservation demanded she get rid of him ASAP.

'Thanks for dinner and driving me home,' she said, juggling her handbag from one arm to the other, hoping he'd get the hint.

'My pleasure.' He stilled her arm with a light touch on the forearm. 'Not going to invite me in?'

She admired his bluntness. But she hated being put on the spot.

'I don't think that's a good idea.'

His hand travelled up her arm in a slow caress before resting on her shoulder. 'Why? Scared we'll have a repeat of that night at the hotel?'

'No. I just have a lot of work to do before my meeting with Danni tomorrow so—'

He kissed her, a stealth kiss that caught her completely off guard.

Her hands braced against his chest, ready to push him away as he backed her up against the front door.

But then his tongue touched her bottom lip, stroked it with exquisite precision, and she clung to him instead. Responded to his commanding mouth, deepening the kiss to sublimely erotic, craving more.

When his arms slid around her waist and pulled her flush against him, her body zinged with remembrance. How it felt to be pressed against his erection, how he'd masterfully seduced her with a skill that left her breathless, weightless, floating, as he kissed like a guy who couldn't get enough. The feeling was entirely mutual.

When Wade kissed her, when he touched her, she forgot about responsibilities. She forgot about the stress of losing her money and Cindy's security. She forgot about the long list of doctor's appointments and physiotherapy sessions and hydrotherapy at a new pool next week. She forgot about finding a replacement carer for when Shar went on vacation next.

She existed purely in the moment, revelling in this incredibly sexy guy's desire for her.

As the blood fizzed in her veins and her muscles melted, she wanted more than this kiss.

She wanted him. Naked. Again. The thrill of skin to skin. The excitement of exploring each other's bodies. The release that left her boneless and mindless.

Until a massive reality check in the form of her buzzing phone switched to silent vibrated against her hip.

Shar probably wanted to head home and Liza had momentarily forgotten her responsibilities, indulging in a pointless kiss that could lead nowhere.

Regret tempered her passion as she eased away. The last thing she needed was for Wade to think something was wrong and want to talk, or demand answers she wasn't prepared to give.

'I warned you I wouldn't give up,' he said, cupping her cheek in a tender moment before stepping away.

'You should,' she said, but her words fell on deaf ears as he shot her one, last wicked grin before strolling down her path like a guy who had all the time in the world to woo the woman he wanted.

* * *

An hour later, Liza had bathed Cindy, assisted with her stretches, and helped her painstakingly make a batch of choc-chip muffins.

Every task took double the time with Cindy's clawed elbow and hand but that never stopped her sister from trying anything. At nineteen, her sister planned on opening a digital store selling printable products and had spent countless hours over the last year researching meticulously what that entailed. Liza's admiration knew no bounds and whenever she felt her patience fraying she tried to put herself in Cindy's shoes.

Being a carer over the years had been tough, but imagine being on the receiving end. Being dependent on others for activities of daily living that everyone took for granted. Needing help with bathing and dressing, cooking, and cleaning. Not to mention the never-ending rounds of therapy and medical interventions.

Liza had it easy compared to her sister and Cindy's amazing resilience and zest for life drove her to be a better person every day.

'Were you talking to someone outside?'

The spatula in Liza's hand froze in mid-air, dropping a big globule of muffin mix into the baking tin involuntarily.

'No one important,' she said, concentrating on filling the tin while Cindy popped choc chips into her mouth and chewed slowly.

'Sounded like a guy.' Cindy finished chewing and started making smooching noises.

Uh-oh. Shar had said they'd been busy in the kitchen when she'd arrived home but what if Cindy had seen that kiss?

'You should have a boyfriend,' Cindy said, her wobbly grin endearing. 'A proper one this time, not like those loser sports guys.'

Liza loved that about Cindy, her insightfulness. Most people saw the wheelchair and her physical disfigurement and assumed she was brain-damaged too. While some with cerebral palsy did suffer a degree of brain injury, Cindy had been lucky that way and she often made pronouncements that would've shocked most scholars.

'I'm too busy with my new job to date, sweetie.'

A half-truth, because the guy who wanted to date her happened to work alongside her. It could be convenient...if she lost her mind.

No, having Wade practically invite himself in sixty minutes ago reinforced she was doing the right thing in keeping things between them platonic. She didn't want to let him into her life, into Cindy's life, when there was no future.

While Cindy never talked about their folks abandoning them, it would've hurt. The last thing she needed was Cindy bonding with Wade only to have him head back to London.

She wouldn't do that to herself—or Cindy.

'I have a boyfriend.'

Liza smiled, having been alerted to Cindy's latest crush via Shar. 'You do?'

Cindy nodded. 'Liam Hemsworth. He's hot.'

'Personally, I prefer Chris.'

'No way.' Cindy popped another choc chip in her mouth. 'Though I guess that would work out well. They're brothers, we're sisters. Perfect.'

Liza laughed as she opened the oven door and popped the muffins inside. 'Tell you what. You do another ten hamstring stretches and I'll watch *The Hunger Games* with you again for the umpteenth time.'

'Deal.'

As Cindy manoeuvred her wheelchair into the next room, Liza pondered her sister's observation.

You should have a boyfriend.

While she didn't need the complication, for a second she allowed herself to fantasise what it would be like having Wade fill the role.

Chapter Fifteen

Wade's week had been progressing exceptionally well.

Danni had completed the first draft of Liza's biography, the pre-orders were phenomenal, and he'd managed to sneak another dinner with Liza, albeit for business.

This time she'd driven herself so had avoided his plans for more than a goodnight kiss on her doorstep. He didn't know whether to be peeved or glad she was so focused on her new job.

Considering he'd had his doubts about her when she secured this job, and her motivation behind it, he had to admit she'd impressed. Her dedication, her punctuality, and her fresh ideas had given him new perspective on an industry he'd thought he knew inside out. She was the consummate professional and almost made him feel guilty for constantly picturing her naked.

Almost.

They'd been too busy to catch up beyond snatched marketing meetings in the office and, for a guy who normally had his mind on the job twenty-four-seven, he'd found himself seriously distracted.

Those tight pencil skirts she wore were disruptive, despite their sedate colours and modest below-knee length. Those fitted jackets were the epitome of conservative fashionable chic. Those blouses of muted colours barely had a hint of cleavage. But whenever she entered his office he had an immediate flashback to the night he'd seen beneath the clothes and he'd be hard in an instant.

He dated occasionally in London, but no woman had affected his concentration like Liza. Ever.

When Danni had emailed him the first draft of her biography he'd sat up all night devouring it on his e-reader. His obsession with Liza should've been satisfied. Instead, the more he discovered about her, the more she piqued his curiosity.

She'd delivered exactly what he wanted in terms of a tell-all, a juicy tale highlighting behind-the-scenes gossip in the soccer and basketball worlds. She'd changed names to protect the innocent but he knew readers would devour the catfights and hookups and pick-ups, trying to figure out which real-life stars and WAGs inspired her stories.

This book would sell, but her lack of personal details disappointed. She'd glossed over her childhood and teenage years, focusing on the glamorous drama that kicked in when her high-school boyfriend hit the big time.

He should've been glad, because she'd provided the page-turning hot gossip that sold books. But he'd be lying if he didn't admit to wanting to know more—a whole lot more—about the woman behind the fake tan and designer handbags.

If he had insight into what made her tick, he might understand her continued aloofness. Her lack of enthusiasm at pursuing anything beyond a one-night stand surprised him. Not from ego, but for the simple fact they still shared a spark. More than a spark, if the way she'd responded to his kiss seven days ago was any indication.

So why was she holding back?

He wasn't after anything hot and heavy. He'd been upfront with her about exploring a relationship while he was in Melbourne so anything too deep and meaningful wouldn't scare her off.

She'd refused. But her kiss indicated otherwise.

She wanted this as much as he did, which begged the question, why weren't they out at a movie or dinner or at his place right now?

Instead, he had to face his worst nightmare.

With impeccable timing as always, Babs knocked on his door, and he braced for the inevitable awkwardness that preceded any confrontation with his step-mother. Ridiculous, considering she couldn't be more than ten years older than him, if that.

'Wade, darling.' She breezed into his office and made a beeline for him.

'Babs.' His terse response didn't deter her from planting an air kiss somewhere in the vicinity of his cheek.

He preferred it that way. The less those Botoxed lips got near him, the better.

'Thanks for seeing me.' She took a seat without being asked. 'From what I hear we have a lot to catch up on.'

'Really?'

She hated his monosyllabic answers, which was why he did it.

'You're stalling the inevitable.' She waggled a crimson-taloned finger in his direction. 'It would be best for all of us if *Qu Publishing* sold sooner rather than later.'

His fingers dug into the underside of his desk. 'I beg to differ.'

She wrinkled her nose. 'You always did.'

With a calculated pause, she leaned forward and he quickly averted his gaze from her overt cleavage spilling from an inappropriately tight satin blouse.

'It's what your father would've wanted.'

Low blow. Incredibly low. What did he expect? The woman was a gold-digging piranha and probably had already spent the money she'd anticipated from *Qu's* sale.

'My dad would've wanted to see his family legacy live on.' He forced a smile, knowing it would never reach his eyes. 'I'm surprised you wouldn't know that.'

The corners of her mouth pinched, radiating unattractive wrinkles toward her nose. 'We'd both be better off without a struggling business dragging us down. Digital publishing is the way of the future. Audiobooks are booming. Paperbacks are redundant.'

Showed how much she knew. Sure, the digital and audio revolution was a boom for readers but, from the extensive research conducted by online companies over the last five years, there was room in the expanding market for *tree* books, as he liked to call them.

'I have figures to prove you wrong there.' He tapped a stack of documentation on his desk. 'Including record pre-orders for Liza Lithgow's biography.'

'That tart?'

Wade would never touch a woman in anger, would never consider it, but he wouldn't mind clamping a hand over this vile woman's mouth and dragging her out of his office.

Babe nose crinkled like she'd smelled something bad. 'Who would want to read about her fabricated life?'

He wouldn't give her the satisfaction of asking what she meant.

'All those WAGs are the same. Fake, the lot of them. Happy to be arm candy for what they can get.'

Pot. Meet kettle. Wade had heard enough.

'I'm not selling, Babs. The board isn't selling. They've agreed to give me three months to take this company into the black and they are men of honour.'

More than he could say for her. She wouldn't know honour if it jumped up and bit her on her nipped and tucked ass.

Her eyes narrowed, and took on a feral gleam. 'You're pinning the success of this entire company on one book? Not a smart business decision. All sorts of disasters could happen before it hits the bookstores, like—'

'I have to get back to work,' he said, standing and heading for the door, which he opened in a blatant invitation for her to get the hell out of his office.

She stood and strolled toward him, deliberately taking her time. 'I'll be at the next board meeting.'

'I'm sure you will,' he said, resisting the urge to slam the door as she stepped through it.

'What you're doing is wrong and your father would be appalled at the risk you're taking—'

This time he gave into instinct and slammed the door.

Chapter Sixteen

'There's a book launch I want to suss out tonight,' Wade said, barely glancing up from his paperwork. 'We're going.'

Liza bristled. She didn't take kindly to orders, least of all from the man she could happily throttle given half a chance.

He'd been bugging her all week, using subtle charm and sexy smiles to undermine her. She'd weathered it all, had focused on work in the hope he'd forget this ridiculous challenge of trying to woo her.

He hadn't, until today. Today, he'd been brusque and abrupt to the point of rudeness and no one seemed to know why. She should've been happy. Instead, a small part of her missed his roguish charisma.

'*We* may have other plans,' she said, in a manufactured sickly sweet voice.

He glanced up, the frown between his brows not detracting from his perfection. 'A rival company is releasing a soap-opera starlet's biography. It pays to scope out the competition, get a few ideas for what works at these shindigs and what doesn't.'

Liza hated the hint of deflation she felt that his command had been pure business and not a burning desire to spend some time in her presence outside work.

Crazy and contradictory, considering that's the last thing she wanted and she had gone to great pains to avoid any out-of-work contact since that kiss on her doorstep.

But a small part of her, the part that reluctantly dredged up memories of their scintillating night together, yearned for a repeat.

Needless to say that part of her didn't get acknowledged these days.

'Surely you've been to heaps of book launches? What's so special about this one?'

With an exasperated sigh, he flung his pen on top of the towering stack of paperwork threatening to topple.

'I've heard they're trying an innovative giveaway. Something along the lines of buy the book, get a download of another free.' He pushed aside the paperwork with one hand and pinched the bridge of his nose with the other. 'I want to see how well it's received by readers who prefer to hold a tree book.'

'Tree book?'

His mouth relaxed into a semi-smile. 'Paper comes from trees. Paperbacks? Tree books.'

'Cute,' she said, a broad term that could be applied to his terminology or the man himself when he lost the 'shouldering the weight of the company on my shoulders' look.

He'd been grumpy all day but she'd weathered it, assuming he had profit margins to juggle or worry about. Having him crack a half-smile was a big improvement.

'My dad used to call them that,' he said, interlinking his fingers and stretching overhead. It did little to ease the obvious tension in his rigid shoulders.

'He built an incredible company,' she said, surprised by his rare information sharing.

While Wade seemed content to interrogate her, his personal life was definitely off-limits. The snippets she'd learned about the enigmatic CEO had come from colleagues, co-workers who'd given her the lowdown on *Qu Publishing*. A company founded sixty years ago by Wade's grandfather, a company that had produced many bestsellers under Wade's dad, but a company that had floundered when Wade's step-mother had entered the picture and Wade had left to start his own company in London.

While no one would directly disparage Babs Urquart, Liza saw enough glowering expressions and heard enough half-finished sentences to know Babs wasn't well liked.

Apparently they blamed her for Qu's downfall. And so did their boss.

'You started out here too?'

His lips compressed, as if he didn't want to talk about it. 'Yeah. I left after a few years, started my own company in London.'

'Bet your dad was proud.'

'Yeah, though we lost touch over the last few years.' Pain flickered in his eyes and she wished she hadn't probed. 'We caught up infrequently in person. Snatched phone calls here and there.'

He shook his head, the deep frown slashing his brow indicative of a deeper problem. It looked as if she wasn't the only one with parental issues. 'I resent that distance between us now. He had a heart condition and didn't tell me until it was too late.'

Appalled, Liza resisted the urge to hug him. 'Why?'

Wade shrugged. It did little to alleviate the obvious tension making his neck muscles pop. 'I guess he didn't trust me to be there for him, considering I'd deliberately distanced myself from him.'

Liza didn't know what to say. She despised trite platitudes, the kind that Cindy copped from ignorant, condescending people. And it was pretty obvious Wade had major guilt over his relationship with his dad, so nothing she could say would make it any better.

But she knew what it was like to be let down by a parent, knew the confusing jumbled feelings of pain and regret and anger.

'Kids and parents grow apart. Maybe it wasn't so much a lack of trust in you that he didn't mention his heart condition and more a case of not wanting to worry you because he cared?'

Wade's startled expression spoke volumes. He'd never considered that might've been his dad's rationale.

'So you're a glass-half-full girl?'

'Actually, I'm a realist rather than an optimist.' She had to be, because it was easier to accept the reality of her life than wish for things that would never eventuate. 'And whatever or whoever caused the rift between you, it's not worth a lifetime of guilt.'

His steady gaze, filled with hope, didn't leave hers. 'I should've been there for him and I wasn't.'

A mantra taken from her mum's handbook to life, too.

'He loved you, right?'

Wade nodded.

'Then I think you have your answer right there.' She tapped her chest. 'If it was my heart and I had people I cared about, I'd rather make the most of whatever time we had together, even if it was only phone calls, than field a bunch of useless questions like "How are you feeling?" or "Is there anything I can do?"'

She lowered her hand and continued. 'I wouldn't care about how often I saw the person or waste time worrying over trivial stuff like the length of time since we spoke. I'd remember the good times and want to live every minute as if it were my last.'

'Dad did travel a lot the last two years...' He straightened, his frown clearing. 'Thanks.'

Uncomfortable with his praise and wishing she hadn't blabbed so much, she shrugged. 'For what? Being a philosophising pragmatist?'

'For helping me consider another point of view.' Wade gestured at the office. 'Dad did a great job building this company and we were close. Until he got distracted.'

His frown returned momentarily and she knew it would take more than a few encouraging words from her to get him to change his mindset and let go of the guilt.

Deliberately brusque and businesslike, he shuffled papers on his desk. 'I'm here to ensure the company regains a foothold in the publishing market.'

'I thought that's why I'm here.'

She'd hoped to make him laugh. Instead, he fixed her with a speculative stare.

'How do you do it?'

'Do what?'

'Live your life under a spotlight. Fake it for all those people.'

Increasingly uncomfortable, she shrugged. 'Who said I was faking?'

He ran a hand over his face. 'Something my annoying stepmother said, about WAGs leading fabricated lives.'

A shiver of foreboding sent a chill through Liza. What the hell was that supposed to mean? Did Babs Urquart know something? Or was she making a sweeping generalisation?

Hell, if her fabricated life ever became known they were sunk and Wade would look at her with derision and scorn, not the continued interest that made her squirm with longing.

'Guess we all put on a front when we need to,' she said, thankful her voice didn't quiver. 'Nothing wrong with it if no one gets hurt.'

He didn't reply and his stare intensified.

'Is that what you're doing with me?' He placed his palms on the desk and leaned forward, shrinking the space between them. 'Putting on a front?'

Smart guy.

'Why would I do that?'

Hopefully, he'd buy her feigned innocence.

'Because you're running scared. I want to date you, and I'm pretty damn sure you want to date me, but we continue to do the avoidance dance.' He beckoned her closer with a crooked finger. 'What I want to know is why.'

The longer he stared at her, his dark eyes intent and mesmerising, the harder it was to remember the question let alone formulate an articulate answer.

'Already told you. We work together. It's too complicated.'

She tried to control her choppy breathing, as if her lungs squeezed tight and wouldn't let the air out fast enough. Her excuse for the breathlessness constricting her chest and she was sticking to it.

'Technically, we don't work together. I'm here in the interim. You blackmailed me into giving you a job.' He waved a hand between them. 'You and me? We don't exactly fit the mould of corporate colleagues who shouldn't fraternise.'

He wore the smile of a smug victor. 'Got any other excuses?'

Yeah, Liza had plenty, but she'd never divulge the real reason she couldn't date Wade. Not in a million years.

'For now, don't we have a book launch to attend?' She stood, putting some much-needed distance between them. 'How's that for an excuse?'

'Damn flimsy, if you ask me,' he said, his gaze sweeping over her in admiration.

'I didn't.' She swept up her portfolio and tucked it under her arm. 'Email me the book-launch details and I'll meet you there.'

His frown returned. 'It's two blocks away. Makes sense for us to go together.'

When she took too long to respond, he added, 'I'll walk you back to your car afterwards. You know, in case you think I'll bundle you into my car and try to take advantage of you.'

She couldn't help but laugh. 'Okay.'

Wade shook his head. 'You're an exasperating woman, but if your marketing skills are half as good as your biography, *Qu Publishing* is going to love you.'

Her heart gave a funny little quirk at the L word tripping so easily from his lips. As long as his publishing company was the only thing that loved her. Because as much as Liza secretly yearned for Wade, she didn't have room in her life for love.

Not now.

Not ever.

Chapter Seventeen

'Did you learn anything new at the book launch?'

'Yeah.' Wade screwed up his nose and rubbed his chest. 'Cab Sav and spinach-feta quiche don't mix.'

Liza laughed. 'That'll teach you for eating an entire tray of *hors d'oeuvres.*'

'I didn't have dinner. I was hungry.' The corners of his mouth curved. 'Your fault.'

'How do you figure that?'

'You wouldn't have dinner with me.'

She rolled her eyes. 'That's because you said we had a book launch to attend. For *work*. Remember?'

He sighed. 'Believe me, it's all I think about.'

He took her hand as they entered the underground car park. 'Next to you, that is.'

An illicit thrill shot through Liza. She shouldn't be so happy Wade ranked her next to his precious business, not when she was determined to keep him at bay, but she couldn't help it. The guy was seriously hot and she'd bet he invaded her thoughts a heck of a lot more than she did his.

'We're not supposed to do this for a million reasons—'

'Can't think of one right now.'

He'd pinned her against the wall before she could blink and plastered his mouth to hers.

The feel of his commanding lips wiped all rational thought from her mind as her body responded on an innate level that scared the hell out of her.

With this one, scorching kiss, she remembered in excruciatingly vivid detail how he'd kissed his way all over her body.

How he'd caressed and stroked until she'd been out of her mind.

How he'd licked and savoured every inch of her skin until she'd melted.

His hands slid over her butt and pulled her flush against him.

Damn, how could something so wrong feel so right?

Liza wriggled, needing to push him off, get in her car, and head home to Cindy. Instead, as he changed the pressure of the kiss and touched his tongue to hers, she combusted.

She arched against him, revelling in the feel of his hardness. She speared her fingers through his hair, angled his head, and kissed him right back, pouring every ounce of her repressed yearning into it.

He groaned. She moaned. His hands everywhere, her skin blistering with the heat generated between their bodies.

He didn't stop. She didn't care. Until the sound of a car engine starting on the level below penetrated the erotic fog clouding her head, and she realised what the hell she was doing.

She broke the kiss and dragged in great lungfuls of air, her ragged breathing matching his.

'Don't expect me to apologise for that,' he said, resting his forehead against hers, his hands clasping her waist and leaving her no room to move.

'I would, if I hadn't enjoyed it so much.' She rested her palms on his chest, wishing she had the willpower to shove him away. 'You won't take no for an answer, will you?'

He straightened and smiled down at her. 'You're only just figuring that out?'

'Maybe I'm a slow learner.'

'Or maybe you're running from something when it'd be better to confront it and grab it with both hands?' He squeezed her waist. 'By *it* I mean you should be grabbing *me,* of course.'

Laughter bubbled up in her chest and spilled out. She loved an intelligent guy. She loved a funny guy more. Love being figurative.

'I really need to get home and work on the marketing campaign.'

'And I really need to get home and work on it too.' He released her and snapped his fingers. 'Here's a thought. Why don't we head home together and do some *work?*'

She chuckled. 'Don't hold your breath expecting me to ask your place or mine.'

'Not happening, huh?'

She shook her head. 'No.'

He ducked his head, nuzzled her neck, and the buzz was back. 'There's nothing I can do to change your mind?'

Her libido whimpered and rolled over.

'Uh...no,' she said, too soft, too breathy, too needy.

'Sure?'

His lips brushed the tender skin beneath her ear and

trailed slowly downward where his teeth nipped her collarbone with gentle bites that made her body zing and heat pool low in her belly.

Sure? She wasn't sure of anything, least of all how she would walk to her car, get in, and drive home without him in the passenger seat.

'Wade, you're so—'

'Addictive?' He licked the dip between her collarbones.

'Wicked?' He deliberately brushed his stubbled jaw along the top of her breast.

'Sexy?' He edged toward her mouth, his lips teasing at the corner.

'Persistent,' she said, holding her breath as his lips brushed hers once, twice, soft, taunting.

As a car's headlights panned over them, Liza nudged him away. 'This would be a great boost for the book's marketing. *CEO and WAG caught in compromising position underground carpark.*'

'All publicity's good publicity,' he said, completely unruffled while she felt dishevelled and flustered and turned on.

'Beg to differ.' She tugged down her jacket, straightened her blouse, and smoothed her hair. 'Are you walking me to my car or not?'

'Lead the way.' His arm swept forward in a flourish and as she passed him she could've sworn his hand deliberately brushed her butt.

Wade didn't play fair.

Then again, the way her skin tingled with awareness and her body lit up from within, did she want him to?

Chapter Eighteen

Despite the urge to run from Wade as fast as her legs could carry her, Liza was glad he'd walked her to her car.

She wouldn't have made it otherwise. Her knees shook so badly after their impromptu make-out session in a dark corner of the underground car park, if it hadn't been for his steadying arm around her waist she would've definitely stumbled. And her head was shrouded in a passionate haze, her only excuse for slipping up and not waving him away before they reached her car.

'You drive *this?*'

She slipped out of his grasp and fumbled for her keys. 'Yeah, why?'

'I pictured you in something swift and sporty.' Bemused, he walked around her ten-year-old people carrier. 'You could fit an entire football team in the back of this thing.'

Or a wheelchair, but that was on a strictly need-to-know basis.

'I like big cars.' She tried not to sound defensive and failed, if his raised eyebrows were any indication.

'So it seems.'

She flicked the remote button to unlock the doors but he laid a hand on her forearm and stopped her from opening the driver's door.

'Wait.'

She couldn't, because if she spent one more second around him she'd fall into his arms and beg for a repeat of that one memorable night they'd spent together.

'I really have to go.'

In response, he moved in closer, placing a hand either side of her waist and pinning her between cold, hard metal behind and hot, hard body in front.

'Come home with me.'

Her heart lurched with longing but before she could protest he rushed on. 'You doubted my sincerity the first night we were together? Then let's start afresh. Make tonight our night. No work. No excuses. Just two people who are crazy about each other indulging their mutual passion.'

His heated gaze bore into her, unrelenting, demanding an honest answer. 'No complications at the office tomorrow. No second-guessing. Just you and me, and an incredible night to be ourselves.'

Liza was tempted. Beyond tempted. Her body strained toward him of its own volition, miles ahead of her head in saying yes. But what was the point? One more night would only solidify what she already knew.

She could easily fall for Wade Urquart given half a chance.

But she couldn't. Not with her responsibilities. Not with her life plan. It wouldn't be fair to encumber a guy with Cindy's full-time care and she would never leave Cindy to fend for herself. It was why she never considered a long-term relationship, why she would never marry.

Normally, it didn't bother her. But she'd never met a guy like Wade before, the kind of guy who elicited wild fantasies, the kind that consisted of homes and picket fences and a brood of dark-haired, dark-eyed cherubs just like their dad.

'Stop thinking so hard.' He placed a hand over her heart and it bucked wildly beneath it. 'What does this tell you?'

To run like the wind. But she swallowed that instinctive response and reluctantly met his gaze.

She had to refuse.

But an incredible thing happened as her eyes met his. She saw a confusing jumble of hope and vulnerability and desire, every emotion she was feeling reflected back at her like a mirror.

No guy she'd ever been with had been so revealing and in that moment she knew she couldn't walk away from him. At least for tonight.

'Okay,' she said, mimicking his action and feeling his heart pound beneath her palm. 'But this is a one-off, okay? We don't discuss it again or bring it up at the office.'

'Okay,' he said, swooping in for a kiss that snatched her breath and quite possibly her heart.

Liza didn't remember much of the short drive to Wade's Southbank apartment. She could barely concentrate on the road with his hand on her thigh the entire time.

He didn't speak, sensing her need for silence. She couldn't speak, not without the risk of blurting how he made her feel. Uncertain and flustered and high.

Hell, how bad would it be come morning after another amazing night in his arms?

She shouldn't have agreed, but the part of her that had the life she'd planned ripped away following the phone call from her financial adviser's office still craved a little indulgence.

She was doing her best: with the biography, with the marketing job, with caring for Cindy. She deserved a break, deserved to feel good, and Wade was guaranteed to make her feel incredible albeit for a few hours tonight.

His penthouse apartment was everything she'd imagined: glossy wooden floors, electric controlled slimline blinds, glass and chrome and leather everywhere. Minimalist chic, reeking of money.

Not that he gave her much of a chance to study it, because the moment they stepped down into the split-level living room he had his arms around her and backed her against a sleek marble-topped table.

'Do you have any idea how much I want you?' He framed her face with his hands, staring deep into her eyes.

The depth of his need shocked her, as if he'd given her a glimpse into his soul. He shouldn't want her this much. It wouldn't end well. But she'd come too far to back out now and she couldn't if she wanted to. She needed him just as badly, if only for tonight.

'I have a fair idea,' she said, undulating her hips against the evidence of how badly he wanted her.

He growled. 'Tease.'

'No, a tease would do this.'

Her hands splayed against his chest, caressed upward before stroking downward. Lower. And lower. Stopping short of his belt buckle.

'A tease would also do this.' She slowly slid the leather belt out, toying with the buckle.

'And this.' She flicked the top button of his pants open.

The PLAYER

'A tease would stop here.' She inched his zipper down, the sound of grating metal teeth the only sound apart from his ragged breathing.

'But I'm no tease.' She pushed his pants down. Slid a hand inside his black boxers. Cupped his cock.

His groan filled the air and, empowered, she went for broke.

He let her undress him until he was standing before her, gloriously naked, incredibly beautiful.

Bronze skin, rippling muscles, hard for her.

'One of us is way overdressed,' he said, taking a step toward her.

'Wait.' She braced a hand on his chest. 'I'm admiring the view.'

'Later,' he said, bundling her into his arms. 'Much later.'

Chapter Nineteen

Lucky for Wade, he'd never had much of an ego.
If he did, it would be smarting.
Liza had done it again. Indulged in a wild, passionate, no-holds-barred night of mind-blowing sex. And then...nothing.

The next day at the office, four weeks ago, she'd reverted to the cool, dedicated woman who'd wowed him with her business ethic that first day she'd presented her marketing ideas. She acted like nothing had changed so he followed her lead, and they'd been nothing beyond courteous colleagues for the last month.

Admittedly, they'd been incredibly busy, with her biography having the fastest turnaround he'd ever seen in all his years in publishing. To have a book written, copy-edited, line-edited, final proofed, and in ARC format within a month? Unheard of, but he'd made it happen. He owed his dad that much. Preserving a family legacy might be the reason everyone assumed was behind his drive to save the company.

Only he knew the truth. Guilt was a powerful motivator.

Despite Liza's encouraging insights that his dad had loved him and that's why Quentin hadn't shared the truth about his heart condition, Wade knew better.

His dad had known how much he despised Babs, but he'd been too much of a gentleman to bring it up or let it effect their relationship initially. But with Wade's continued withdrawal, both physically and emotionally, he'd irrevocably damaged the one relationship he'd ever relied on.

His dad not trusting him enough to divulge the truth about his heart condition before it was too late hurt, deeper than he'd ever imagined.

He regretted every moment he'd lost with his dad. Regretted all the time they could've spent together if he'd known the truth. Regretted how he'd let his superiority, judgement, and distaste for Babs ruin a friendship that surpassed a simple father-son bond. Most of all, he regretted not having the opportunity to say a proper goodbye.

He'd regret it all and the rift he'd caused until his dying day, but for now he'd do everything in his power to ensure *Qu* thrived as a token of respect for the man who had given him everything.

He had the woman who'd sold her story to him to thank too.

Wade had done as she suggested over the last few weeks. Remembered the good times with his dad: authors they'd signed together, books they'd published that had gone on to hit bestseller lists, a patient Quentin teaching him golf as a teenager and the many hack games that had followed over the years, the beers they'd share while watching the motor sport.

So many precious memories he'd deliberately locked away because of the hurt. But Liza had been right. Holding onto guilt only made it fester and remembering the good times had gone some way to easing his pain.

She'd given him a wake-up call he needed and had a surprise as a thank you.

He knocked on Liza's door, holding the Advanced Reader Copy behind his back. He hoped she'd be as thrilled with how her story had turned out as he was.

He'd stayed up all night, devouring Liza's biography from cover to cover. When he'd speed read the first draft in e-format he'd done so with an editor's eye and hadn't really had time to absorb the facts beyond she'd delivered the juicy tell-all he'd demanded.

After reading the ARC last night, holding her life in *tree* format, he'd felt closer to her somehow, as if learning snippets from her childhood revealed her to him in a way she'd never do in person.

Of course, he'd hated her dating tales, insanely jealous of the soccer and basketball stars that had wooed her and whisked her to parties and elite functions, living the high life. Irrational, because he had no reason to be jealous; those guys were her past.

But was he her future?

Damned if he knew. It wasn't as if they were looking for anything long term. He'd spelled it out at the start and Liza had done her best to maintain her distance when they weren't burning up the sheets those two times.

So why the intense disappointment she'd been willing to share part of her life with him, but only for the money?

The door opened and a forty-something woman with spiked blonde hair, no makeup, and sporting a frown eyed him up and down. 'Yes?'

'Hi, Wade Urquart, here to see Liza.'

The woman's eyes widened as a sly smile lit her face. 'Nice to meet you, Wade. I'm Shar. Come on in.'

Shar ushered him through the door and it took a moment to register two things.

A pretty young woman bearing a strong resemblance to Liza was engrossed in a jigsaw puzzle alongside Liza.

The young woman was in a wheelchair.

Their heads turned as one as he stepped into the room, the young woman's lopsided welcoming smile indicative of some kind of disability, Liza's stunned expression a mix of horror and fear.

It confused the hell out of him.

Why was she horrified to see him? Was she scared he'd run a mile because she had a disabled relative, probably a sister?

The possibility that she thought so little of him irked.

He strode forward, determined to show her he was ten times the man she gave him credit for.

'Hi, I'm Wade.' He stuck out his hand, waiting for the young woman to place her clawed hand in his, and shook it gently.

'Cindy, Liza's sister,' she said, her blue eyes so like Liza's, bright with curiosity and mischief. 'Are you Liza's boyfriend?'

'Yes,' he said, simultaneously with Liza's, 'No.'

Shar smothered a laugh from behind. 'Come on, Cindy, let's leave these two to sort out their confusion.'

Cindy chuckled and Wade said, 'Nice meeting you both,' as they left the room.

Liza stood, her movements stiff and jerky as she rounded the table, arms folded. 'What are you doing here?'

'I came to give you this.'

He handed her the ARC, his excitement at sharing it with her evaporating in a cloud of confusion. Why hadn't she told him about her sister Cindy? Did he mean that little to her?

They might not have a solid commitment or long-term plans but he'd thought they'd connected on a deeper level beyond the physical. At the very least they were friends, and friends shared stuff like this.

As her fingers closed around the creased spine from his rapid page-turning the night before, the truth detonated.

His hand jerked back and the ARC fell to the floor with a loud thud.

'There's no mention of Cindy in your bio.'

She glared at him, defiant. "Of course not. I don't want the whole world knowing about my sister—'

'What the—?' He ran a hand over his face, hoping it would erase his disgust, knowing it wouldn't. 'You're embarrassed by her.'

She stepped back as if he'd struck her, her mouth a shocked O.

Anger filled him, ugly and potent. He didn't know what made him madder: that she'd lied in her bio, that she was ashamed of her sister, or that she hadn't trusted him enough to tell him anything.

He kicked at the ARC. 'Is any of this true?'

She flinched. 'My life is between those pages—'

'Bullshit.' He lowered his voice with effort. 'Leaving your sister out of your biography is a major twisting of the truth. Which makes me wonder, what else have you lied about?'

He waited for her to deny his accusation, desperately wanted her to, but she stood there, staring at him with sorrow and regret, and he had his answer.

'I could lose everything,' he said, anger making his hands shake. His fingers curled into fists and he shoved them into his pockets. 'The bulk of your advance came out of my pocket. Three hundred grand's worth.'

He should feel more panicky about the precarious position he'd placed his own company in to save his dad's—the advance was only the start, because he'd poured another half a million into the marketing budget for the biography too—but all he could think about was how Liza had lied to him. How she'd withheld the truth from him.

Just like his dad.

He'd told her about Quentin not trusting him enough, about how it affected him. Hell, she'd even given him that pep talk.

Yet she'd gone and done the same regardless.

'I earned that advance.' Her flat monotone made him want to shake her to get some kind of reaction. 'I gave you the story you wanted.'

'So what? I should be grateful?' His bitterness made her flinch. 'I should've known better than to trust someone like you.'

She paled but didn't say anything, her lack of defence riling him further.

'Guess you played me like those other poor suckers in your *biography*,' he said, not proud of the low blow but lashing out, needing to hurt her as much as she'd hurt him.

That's when the real truth detonated.

He wouldn't care this much, wouldn't be hurting this much, if he hadn't fallen for her.

A woman who didn't trust him, a woman who thought nothing of their developing relationship, a woman who'd done all of this for the money only.

Reeling from the realisation, he did the only thing possible.

Turned on his heel, strode out of the door, and slammed it behind him.

Chapter Twenty

Liza sank onto the nearest chair and clutched her stomach, willing the rolling nausea to subside.

She didn't know what was worse: feeling as if she was about to hurl or the breath-snatching ache in her chest.

This was why she never let any guy get too close.

This was why she never should've let Wade into her life.

And into her heart.

Despite every effort to push him away and keep their relationship strictly business, he'd bustled his way in with charm and panache and flair. And she'd let him.

She knew why too. Because for the first time in forever she'd felt cherished. Spoiled. As if someone was looking out for her rather than the other way around.

She didn't mind being Cindy's carer but for a brief interlude in her life Wade had swept her off her feet and taught her what it felt like being on the other side.

'Double mocha or double-choc-fudge brownies?' Shar bustled into the room, pretending not to look at her while casting concerned glances out of the corner of her eye as she tidied up a stack of magazines.

'Both,' Liza said, knowing she'd be unable to stomach either but needing a few more minutes alone to reassemble her wits.

'Okay. Back in a sec.'

Breathing a sigh of relief, Liza eased the grip on her stomach and stretched. Rolled her shoulders. Tipped her neck from side to side. It did little for the tension making her muscles twang but at least she wouldn't get a spasm on top of everything else.

Wade had ousted her lies. Worse, he thought she was ashamed of Cindy, when nothing could be further from the truth. And the fact he hadn't let her explain, had stood there and hurled accusations at her, hurt.

Maybe she should've trusted him with the truth. But her motives had been pure. She'd done it all for Cindy. Would do it again if it meant protecting her sister.

Now he knew the truth, where did that leave them?

'Here you go.' Shar dumped a plate of brownies and a steaming mocha in front of her. 'Looks like you could do with a good dose of chocolate.'

'You heard?' Liza picked at the corner of a brownie, and shoved a few crumbs around the plate with her fingertip.

'Enough.' Shar winced. 'It didn't sound good.'

'Is Cindy okay?'

Shar nodded. 'Yeah, she's on the computer listening to a podcast by that social media influencer she raves about, so had her headphones on.'

'Guess I should be grateful for small mercies,' Liza said, the severity of her confrontation with Wade hitting home at the thought of Cindy overhearing what he'd accused her of.

Star stared at her, a frown grooving her brow. 'You didn't tell him about Cindy.'

It was a statement, not a question, and Liza didn't know where to begin to rationalise her behaviour.

'He seems like a nice guy.' Shar sipped at her mocha. 'Good looking too.'

'Wade's...' What? Incredibly sexy? Persistent? Thoughtful? She settled for the truth. 'Special.'

'Then why all the secrecy?'

'Because I wanted to protect Cindy.'

'From?'

'Prying. Interference.'

'Ridicule?' Shar prompted and Liza nodded, biting her bottom lip.

'You'll probably hate me for saying this, but are you sure it's Cindy you were protecting and not you?'

Liza's head snapped up, shocked by Shar's accusation. 'What do you mean?'

Shar screwed up her nose before continuing. 'You've lived your life in the spotlight. Interviews on TV. Mingling with A-listers. Your life scrutinised online. Best parties. Best of everything.'

Shar paused, and glanced away. 'Maybe you didn't want people knowing you had a disabled sister because you thought it would taint how you appear to others in some way?'

'That's bull.' Liza stood so quickly her knee knocked the underside of the table and she swore.

'Then why are you so defensive?'

She glared at Shar. 'Because what you've just suggested is hateful and makes me look like a narcissistic bitch.'

Shar shook her head. 'No. It makes you human.'

Shar's accusation made Liza pause. Had that partially

been her motivation? Was Wade right? Was she ashamed to reveal to the world she had a disabled sister?

Never in a million years would she have thought that, but if the two people in the world she was closest to—discounting Cindy—had jumped to the same conclusion, had she done it on some subconscious level?

She collapsed back onto the chair and tried to articulate her jumbled feelings. 'Because of what I've faced in the spotlight, I didn't want Cindy exposed to any of that.'

Shar pointed at the ARC lying on the floor. 'So what if you'd mentioned her in the book? Doesn't mean the media would've been beating down your door to interview her.'

'They might have.' Liza rested her feet on the chair and wrapped her arms around her shins. 'You've fielded enough calls to know how persistent they can be. It could've turned into a circus.'

'Or they could've respected your privacy and hers.'

Liza blew a raspberry. 'I hate it when you're logical.'

Shar winked. 'All part of the service.'

Now that Liza had come this far, she should tell Shar all of it.

'I did it for the money.'

'The biography?'

Liza nodded. 'That day I went to *Qu Publishing* to tell them to stop harassing us, I had a phone call from my financial adviser's office.'

She took a deep breath, blew it out. 'My investment has gone. He scammed the lot.'

Shar blanched. 'Hell, that's diabolical.'

'To put it mildly.' Liza hugged her knees tighter. 'I was still in the office when I took the call, after basically telling Wade to stick his offer to publish my biography. But after I got the news,

I was reeling. Wade found me in a crumpled heap and was a good sport, so in the end, I had to accept his offer. The advance and royalties from the biography were the only way out.'

'Drastic times call for drastic measures.' Shar picked up the ARC from the floor and laid it on the table. 'If you didn't mention Cindy in the book, did you stretch the truth in general?'

'A little.' Liza wavered a hand side to side. 'I mostly stuck to the truth with the WAG side of things. Played up all that glamorous nonsense people lap up. It's what he asked for.'

'What about your folks?'

'I told the truth. Within reason.'

Even now, ten years after her mum had walked out on them, and almost two decades since her dad had bolted too, Liza cushioned the hurt by justifying their appalling behaviour. They didn't deserve it but the last thing she needed was for Cindy to realise the truth one day.

That their parents had left because of her.

Cindy had been too young to know their father, had swallowed the story their mum had told—they'd grown apart and divorced—when in reality he'd been a coward, unable to cope with a disabled daughter and had taken the easy way out by abandoning them all.

As for their mum, Cindy wasn't a fool and had been stoic when she'd left. Louisa had emotionally withdrawn for years and Cindy had been philosophical, almost happy, when Liza became her sole carer.

Finding Shar at the time had been a godsend too and Liza knew she wouldn't have made it this far without the full-time carer and confidante.

'As long as you didn't tell blatant lies, I don't see what

the problem is.' Shar picked up the ARC and flipped through it. 'What did he mean about losing everything?'

'Apparently the advance came out of his pocket.'

But from what she'd learned, Wade was loaded. He had his own publishing company in London. Then again, she knew better than anyone that appearances could be deceptive. If his company was anything like *Qu Publishing* and the rest of the industry, maybe he'd taken a hit with the digital boom and was losing millions with falling print runs?

But her biography was already at the printers, ready to ship to the many bookstores that had pre-ordered by the thousands, and those pre-orders were like gold.

So what if she'd omitted Cindy from her story? What the readers didn't know wouldn't hurt them. He'd overreacted, probably smarting more from her omission than any real financial pressure.

Shar laid the ARC on the table and nudged it toward her. 'Maybe you should talk to him?'

'Are you kidding?' Liza shook her head. 'You didn't see how mad he was.'

'Give him time to cool off, then talk to him.' Shar took a huge bite of brownie, chewed it, before continuing. 'Besides, isn't he your boss? You'll have to talk some time.'

Hell. Somewhere between the shock of having him turn up at her house and the kerfuffle of fending off his wild accusations, she'd forgotten she'd have to face him at work and see the devastation and disgust in Wade's eyes all over again.

Shar dusted off her hands. 'Go easy on him. I think he likes you.'

That's where the problem lay.

Liza liked him too.

Too much to be good for her.

The PLAYER

* * *

After helping bathe and dress Cindy, Liza settled into the nightly routine of rubbing moisturiser into Cindy's dry skin.

She loved this special bonding time, when they relaxed and chatted about their respective days. Liza had missed it on the evenings when she'd been on WAG duty. It spoke volumes about her previous lifestyle that she would've rather been home with her sis than partying with a bunch of fake socialites.

'That feels good.' Cindy closed her eyes and rested her head against the back of the chair as Liza spread the moisturiser evenly over her forearm with firm strokes.

'Your skin's looking great,' Liza said, always on the lookout for pressure sores or skin breakdown, common side effects with CP.

'Thanks to you.' Cindy sighed as Liza increased the pressure slightly. 'Wade seems nice.'

'Hmm.' Liza deliberately kept her strokes rhythmic, not wanting to alert Cindy to her sudden spike in blood pressure.

She didn't want to think about Wade now, didn't want to remember the disappointment and censure in his eyes as he'd stalked out two hours ago.

His accusations cut deep. He'd assumed she was ashamed of Cindy...well, screw him. He wouldn't have a clue what it was like for her, trying to keep Cindy calm and avoiding stress that could potentially increase her spasticity.

Liza had seen it happen, any time Cindy was anxious, upset, agitated, or excited. The medical team had advised her to avoid such situations, and that was the main reason Liza hadn't included Cindy in the book.

She couldn't run the risk of people invading Cindy's

privacy, pestering for interviews and potentially increasing the likelihood of those disastrous contractures.

The changes in Cindy's soft tissues terrified Liza. The shortening of muscles, tendons, and ligaments could lead to muscle stiffness, atrophy, and fibrosis, where the muscles become smaller and thinner. And if those muscles permanently shortened and pulled on the nearby bones, the resultant deformities could be a significant problem.

Her sister worked so hard at her exercises but Liza constantly worried about contractures, where the spasticity in Cindy's arm and leg might reach a point where the muscles required surgical release.

Cindy co-operated most days but they'd had their battles over the years, when no amount of cajoling or bribery could get Cindy to follow her exercise regimen.

Liza hated playing taskmaster but she did it. Anything to avoid seeing Cindy in more pain than she already was. Cindy coped with the chronic pain from the abnormal postures of her joints admirably but it broke Liza's heart every time her sister winced or cried out during her routine.

Liza stayed positive and tried to encourage as much as she could, because the possibility of a hip subluxation or scoliosis from the contractures was all too real and she wanted to avoid further medical intervention for Cindy at all costs.

So including her in the biography and having Cindy agitated or overexcited, leading to contractures? No way, Liza couldn't do it. She'd never intentionally hurt her sister or put her in harm's way and that was how she'd viewed revealing Cindy's identity to the world.

As for Shar's insinuation that maybe Liza hadn't wanted to be tainted by Cindy's disability in some way, that was off base. Liza would've loved to raise awareness for cerebral palsy, the association, and the carers, and her tell-all would've been the perfect vehicle.

But Cindy came first always and she couldn't run the risk of her spasticity worsening.

'He said he was your boyfriend.' Cindy's eyes snapped open and pinned Liza with an astute glare she had no hope of evading.

'Guys get confused sometimes.' Liza reached for Cindy's other arm and started the massage process all over again. 'If you smile in their direction they think you're crushing on them.'

Cindy laughed, a sound Liza never tired of. 'Maybe that's the problem? You've been smiling too much at Wade?'

'Could be.'

Though Liza knew smiling would be the last thing happening when they met next. Shar was right. She had to talk to him, had to calm this volatile situation before she lost her job.

And maybe lost the guy, though she had a sinking feeling that had already happened.

Chapter Twenty-One

After the blow-up with Liza, Wade headed for the one place he felt safe.

The office.

It had been his refuge for as long as he could remember, whether in Melbourne or London, the one place he was on top and in total control.

The office he could rely on, whereas family could be as changeable as the wind and his fractured relationship with his father over Babs proved it. Girlfriends, he'd chosen with deliberation, the kind of corporate women who expected nothing and were content with a brief fling, which meant he was close to none of them.

The publishing business had been the one constant in his life, the one thing he could depend on.

Now, courtesy of Liza's lies, he could lose that too.

It had taken a full hour of checking with his legal team and exploring all possible scenarios for him to calm down. Even if Liza's biography wasn't one-hundred-per-cent accurate, according to the contract the readers would have no recourse if the truth of Cindy's existence came out.

The PLAYER

He'd assumed it wouldn't be a problem but needed to know for sure. After all, how many celebrities invented backgrounds and touted it as truth?

In the heat of the moment, when he'd realised she'd kept something as important as her sister from him, he'd snapped and said he could lose everything. He'd thrown it out there to shame her; to intimidate her into telling him the truth—why she'd done it—when in reality the eight hundred grand from his own pocket wouldn't make or break him.

Now that he'd calmed down enough to rationally evaluate the situation, he might not have lost his dad's company but he had lost something equally important.

The woman he loved.

How ironic that the first time he let a woman get closer than dinner and a date, the first time he'd learned what it meant to truly desire someone beyond the physical, had turned into the last time he'd ever be so foolish again.

And a scarier thought: was he like his dad after all? Had Liza played him as Babs had played his dad?

He wouldn't have thought so; the times they'd been intimate had been so revealing, so soul-reaching, he could've sworn she'd been on the same wavelength.

But she'd sought him out at the very beginning. She'd blackmailed her way into a job. Had that been her end game from the start?

Was their relationship a way of keeping him onside while she milked the situation for all it was worth?

After all, she'd done it before. According to her biography—if any of it was true—she'd been thrust into the WAG limelight by default when her high-school sweetheart became pro, but with the basketball star she later dated she implied they'd had an understanding based on a solid friendship and mutual regard.

Yet when he'd studied the pictures of her and Henri Jaillet, her body language spoke volumes. If the cameras were trained on her, Liza stood tall and smiled, while subtly leaning away from Henri's arm draped across her shoulders or waist. In the candid shots, she stood behind Henri, arms folded, shoulders slumped, lips compressed.

Those photos implied she hadn't enjoyed a moment of their relationship yet she'd done it regardless, enduring it for a year.

What had she told him at the start? *'We all do things we don't want to?'*

If so, why? Had it been to support her sister? Had she deliberately thrust herself into the limelight? Had it been for the adulation or was there more behind it?

That was what gutted him most, that he felt closer to her while reading her biography, as if she'd let him into her life a little, when she hadn't let him in at all.

He swirled the whiskey he nursed before downing the amber spirit in two gulps. The burn in his gullet didn't ease the burn in his heart and the warmth as it hit his stomach didn't spread to the rest of him. He'd been icy cold since he left Liza's, unable to equate the woman he'd fallen in love with to the woman who'd hide her disabled sister out of shame.

His door creaked open and he frowned, ready to blast anyone who dared enter. Damn publishing business, one of the few work environments where it wasn't unusual to find employees chained to their desk to meet deadlines at all hours.

'Go away,' he barked, slamming the glass on the side table when the door swung open all the way.

'I said—'

'I heard what you said.' Liza stood in the doorway, framed by the backlight, looking like a person who'd been through an emotional ordeal. He knew the feeling. 'But I'm not going anywhere.'

He swiped a hand over his face. 'I'm not in the mood.'

She ignored his semi-growl, entered the office, and closed the door.

He watched her walk across the office, soft grey yoga pants clinging to her legs, outlining their shape, and desire mingled with his anger. She sat next to him on the leather sofa, too close for comfort, not close enough considering he preferred her on his lap.

Her fingers plucked at the string of her red hoodie, twisting it around and around until he couldn't stand it anymore. He reached out and stilled her hand, watching her eyes widen at the contact before she clasped her hands in her lap.

Great. His touch had become as repugnant as him.

'We need to get a few things straight,' she said, shoulders squared in defiance. 'Firstly, Cindy is the most important person in my life and I'd never be ashamed of her.'

He waited and she glared at him, daring him to disagree.

'Secondly, I've spent most of my life protecting her and that's what my omission was about. Ensuring she wouldn't cop the same crap I have all these years, which may have a detrimental effect on her condition physically.'

'How?'

'Extreme emotions or mood swings can increase the spasticity in her muscles, which in turn can lead to long-term complications. Serious complications that could lead to permanent deformities.'

A tiny sliver of understanding lodged in his hardened heart, cracking it open a fraction, letting admiration creep in. And regret, that he'd unfairly accused her of something so heinous as being ashamed of her sister when she'd been protecting her.

'And thirdly, the rest of my life laid out in the biography is true. Not fabricated. Elaborated? Yeah.' Her fingers twitched, before she unlinked her hands and waved one between them. 'And for the record, what happened between you and I? All real. Every moment, and I'd hate for you to think otherwise.'

Admiration gave way to hope and went a long way to soothing the intense hurt that had rendered him useless until she'd strutted through his door.

But he wouldn't give in that easily. It might have taken a lot of guts to confront him now, so soon after their blow-up, but he couldn't forget that she'd shut him out when he'd let her in.

'Prove it.'

A tiny frown crinkled her brow. 'How?'

'Let me into your life.'

The frown intensified. 'I don't know what you mean.'

'I think you do.' He shuffled closer to her on the couch, buoyed when she didn't move away. 'I want to see the real you. Not the persona you've donned for years to fool the masses. Not the woman you've pretended to be from the beginning of our relationship. The *real* you.'

Liza stared at Wade as if he'd proposed she scale the Eureka Tower naked.

The real her? No one saw the real her, not even Cindy, who she pretended to be upbeat for constantly. The way she saw it, her sister had a tough enough life, why make it harder by revealing when her own life wasn't a bed of roses?

The PLAYER

Liza had always assumed a happy face even if she'd felt like curling up in bed with a romance novel and a pack of Tim Tams.

So what Wade was asking? Too much.

She shook her head. 'I can't—'

'Yes, you can.'

Before she could move, he grasped her hand and placed it over his heart. 'I'm willing to take a chance on us. Without the pretence. Without the baggage of the past. Just you and me. What do you say?'

Chapter Twenty-Two

Liza wanted to run and hide, wanted to fake a smile and respond with a practised retort designed to hide her real feelings.

But looking into Wade's guileless dark eyes, feeling his heart thump steadily, she knew she'd reached a turning point in her life.

She had two options.

Revert to type and continue living a sham.

Or take a giant leap of faith and risk her heart.

'An answer some time this century would be nice,' he said, pressing her hand harder to his heart.

'I'm taking Cindy to Luna Park tomorrow,' she blurted. 'Come with us.'

She waited, holding her breath until her chest ached. She'd never invited anyone to her days out with Cindy. It was their special time. To consider letting Wade accompany them, to see what the reality of being a full-time carer involved, was a huge step forward for her. He wanted to see the real her and she'd thrown down the gauntlet.

His mouth eased into a smile and the air whooshed out of her lungs. 'Sounds good. What time?'

'Nine. We'll pick you up.'

He released her hand to rub his together. 'Great. I get to ride in the people carrier.'

'You're still making jokes about my car, even when you know it's used for a wheelchair?'

He tapped her on the nose. 'Hey, we're genuine from now on, okay? No holding back, no watching what we say. Full disclosure, so I'm teasing you.'

Liza nodded slowly, wondering how he'd feel if he knew all of it.

She didn't have time to find out when he closed the distance between them and kissed her, effectively eradicating all thought and going a long way to soothing the emptiness when he'd walked out earlier.

She hated being abandoned. It dredged up too many painful memories. She never wanted to feel that way again.

* * *

Liza didn't know what she'd expected when she invited Wade to accompany them to Luna Park on the spur of the moment, but a small part of her had probably wanted to test him. To see how he acted around Cindy.

Because when he'd misjudged her initially and made those horrible assumptions about why she hadn't included Cindy in her biography, she'd come to a few realisations. Wade was the only guy she'd ever genuinely cared about and for that reason, after seeing his disgust when she'd withheld the truth, she'd had enough of the lies and the fake life.

She wanted to be herself around him and that included

Cindy. They were a package deal and if he couldn't handle her sister's disability, Liza didn't want to get in any deeper.

Cindy was the deal-breaker.

By the way he'd teased and laughed and chatted with her sister for the last few hours, he'd passed with flying colours.

Liza had seen many people interact with her sister over the years. Some looked away or pretended not to see Cindy. Some stared at her clawed elbow and wrist, at her scissored thighs, at her equinovarus foot. Some patronised by speaking extra slowly or very loudly. Some looked plain uncomfortable.

But from the moment they'd picked up Wade this morning, he'd been at ease with Cindy, treating her like the intelligent nineteen-year-old she was, and in turn, Liza had progressively relaxed as the morning wore on.

She liked not having to pretend around Wade. It was a nice change, not having to fake it all the time. Something she could get used to given half a chance.

While Cindy texted a friend, Wade sat next to Liza and bumped her with his shoulder.

'Having a good time?'

She smiled and nodded. 'Absolutely. I always have a ball when I'm with Cindy.'

'She's amazing,' he said, sliding his hand across her lap to grasp hers. 'And so are you.'

He waved at Cindy with his free hand as she glanced their way. 'Honestly? I don't know a lot about cerebral palsy. I'd planned on researching it last night but got caught up with conference calls.'

Liza admired his interest. Hopefully, it meant his interaction with Cindy today wasn't just a token effort and he genuinely wanted to be involved in Liza's life—which included Cindy too.

'It's a physical disability affecting movement, caused by an injury to the developing brain, usually before birth.'

The corners of his beautiful mouth curved upward. 'You sound like a medical dictionary.'

'With the hours I've spent with doctors and allied health professionals over the years I reckon I could recite an entire medical website.'

'What's her prognosis?'

'Normal life expectancy. The brain damage doesn't worsen as she gets older, but the physical symptoms can.'

As people on the rollercoaster screamed when it plummeted, Cindy glanced up from her phone and laughed, and Liza smiled in response, never tiring of seeing her sister happy.

'Cindy's cerebral palsy is fairly mild. She's diplegic, which means it only affects her arm and leg on one side. And she has spastic CP.'

Wade frowned. 'I hate that word.'

Liza shook her head. 'It's not derogatory. Spasticity means tightness or stiffness of the muscles. The muscles are stiff because the message to move is sent incorrectly to the muscles through the damaged part of the brain.'

'That makes sense.' He frowned, deep in thought. 'Can she walk?'

'A little. At home mainly, in her room, with the aid of a frame. But for Cindy, the harder she works her muscles, the greater the spasticity, so it's easier for her to get around in the wheelchair.'

Liza blew Cindy a kiss as she glanced toward them again and grinned. 'We're definitely lucky. Many cerebral palsy sufferers have intellectual disabilities, speech difficulties, seizures, and severe limitations with eating and drinking. Cindy's main problem is mobility.'

Wade shook his head, as if he couldn't quite believe her optimism. 'You're fantastic.' He nodded toward Cindy. 'The way you are with her is beautiful.'

Uncomfortable with his praise but inwardly preening, she shrugged. 'She's my sister. We've been doing stuff together for a long time.'

'What about your folks?'

She stiffened and he squeezed her hand. 'You glossed over them in your biography and you never mention them...'

Liza didn't want to talk about her flaky folks, not today, not ever. But after Wade's full-disclosure pep talk last night she'd have to give him something.

'I didn't want to make them look bad in the book. That's why I didn't say much beyond the basics.'

He frowned. 'How bad was it?'

'Dad took off when Cindy was a year old. He couldn't handle having a disabled kid. Mum progressively withdrew emotionally over the years, waited until I was eighteen, then she did a runner too.'

Wade swore. 'You've been looking after Cindy ever since?'

'Uh-huh. The CP association hooked me up with Shar shortly after Mum left and she's been a godsend. She's more family than carer.'

More family than her parents combined. The old saying blood was thicker than water? Give her a long, tall glass of clear aqua any day.

'Do you ever hear from them?'

She heard the disapproval in his voice and didn't want to dampen this day. 'Mum calls on birthdays and Christmas, sends money as a gift, that's about it.'

Shock widened his eyes before she saw a spark of understanding. 'That's why you took the book deal, isn't it? You support Cindy financially.'

Liza struggled not to squirm. She didn't want to discuss this with Wade, didn't want him to know her private business.

There was disclosure and there was full disclosure, and as a couple embarking on a possible future, she didn't want to muddy it with her sordid past.

'We do okay,' she said, springing up from the bench and dusting off her butt. 'Come on, I think Cindy's ready for that ice-cream you promised.'

Disappointment twisted his mouth before he forced a smile. 'Sure.'

But as the sun passed behind a cloud and Liza shivered in a gust off Port Phillip Bay, she wondered if her sudden chill had more to do with Wade's obvious disapproval at her reticence than the fickle spring weather.

Chapter Twenty-Three

An hour after Liza dropped him off at the office, Wade strode into the boardroom.

He couldn't get the sound of theme-park rides, Liza's laughter, and Cindy's insightful questions out of his head, or the taste of hot dogs and mint ice-cream off his tongue.

It had been an incredible morning seeing the real Liza for the first time and he'd been blown away by her dedication to her sister, her level of caring, and her sheer joy in spending time with Cindy. She'd revealed a side of her he'd never seen, that of a loving, nurturing sister, and he wondered why she'd gone to great lengths to hide Cindy from him.

Sure, he accepted her rationale about not wanting Cindy exposed to the kind of intrusion she'd faced with her lifestyle over the years, and how emotional swings could increase Cindy's risk factors physically, but there had to be more to it.

He thought she might open up to him today of all days, because he'd seen how she'd looked at him.

The PLAYER

As if she'd really seen him for the first time too.

Her wonder at the way he fit in to her family made him feel ten feet tall, as if he could scale that giant mouth entrance at Luna Park and jog backward on the roller coaster. Then he'd made the fatal mistake of delving deeper and she'd clammed up, shutting him out as if the amazing four hours had never happened.

It confused him, because he had to make some fast decisions regarding his future, and he hoped to have her in it.

He knew what the board were going to say, because he'd received a memo from the chairman late last night after Liza had left the office. Everything he'd worked so hard for, everything his father had achieved, would continue.

He'd saved *Qu Publishing*.

Liza's biography had saved *Qu Publishing*, and rather than taking her out for a night on the town to celebrate, he knew when he broke the news neither of them would feel like champagne.

Achieving his goal of preserving his father's legacy meant the end of his time in Melbourne.

The end of his relationship with Liza before it had really begun.

Now that he'd seen her with Cindy, he knew she'd never leave her sister. She was too dedicated, and he wouldn't ask that of her.

But there was another solution--they could come with him—and he rubbed his temples, excited by the prospect but knowing it would be a big ask.

Liza had outlined clearly what Cindy's medical care involved, so for her to move to another country and have to start all over again with specialists and physiotherapists and a new carer as good as Shar...the chances of her agreeing to move were slim to none.

He couldn't blame her. Liza's love for her sister was all encompassing and he couldn't compete with that. He didn't want to.

But he didn't want their fledgling relationship to end, not when they were finally opening up to each other and investing emotionally.

'Wade?' The chairman slapped him on the back and he dragged in a deep breath, needing to get back in the game.

His personal life could wait. For now, he had a company to solidify.

Wade took his position at the head of the table. 'Thanks for coming, gentlemen.' He mustered a smile for his stepmother. 'Babs.'

Her lips thinned in an unimpressed line.

'As you know, thanks to the pre-orders of Liza Lithgow's biography, *Qu Publishing* has cleared all debts and is firmly in the black. And with projected profit margins from mass market book sales, hardcover, trade paperback, audio, and digital, we're looking at enough capital to ensure viability for years to come.'

He waited until the cheers and clapping died down.

'So I propose a vote. All those in favour of selling *Qu Publishing,* raise your hands.'

There wasn't a flicker of movement at the table as a dozen pairs of eyes stared at him with admiration. All except one, and he glanced at Babs, expecting to see her hand in the air. Surprisingly, she didn't move.

'Well, it looks like the vote is unanimous—'

'I want to say something.' Babs stood and Wade's heart sank. What would she come up with now to derail him?

'Quentin loved this company and I know many of you blame me for distracting him from the office these last few years.'

Gobsmacked, Wade stared at the woman who had far more insight than he'd given her credit for.

'The truth is, Quentin knew he had a heart condition, one that could prove fatal at any time. He wanted to make the most of our time together and I supported that.'

She paused to dab under her eyes, the first time Wade had ever seen her show genuine emotion. 'This company reminds me of what I've lost and that's why I wanted to sell. To move on with my life while holding cherished memories of Quentin.'

Babs' gaze swung toward him. 'Wade, you've done a great job saving this company from the brink, but I want out. You can buy my shares and we'll call it even.'

Wade nodded, startled into silence by this turn of events. He hated hearing Babs articulate his biggest regret: that his dad hadn't shared the seriousness of his prognosis. If he'd known about Quentin's fatal heart condition he never would've wasted so many years staying away because of the woman now looking at him with pity.

He didn't want her pity. He wanted those wasted years back. He wanted to repair the relationship with his dad, the one he'd fractured because of his intolerance. He wanted his dad to trust him enough to tell him the truth.

But he couldn't change the past. He'd have to take control of his future instead and never repeat the same mistakes.

He didn't know if Babs genuinely loved his dad, but he could understand her need to move on with her life. Selling her shares to him would allow them both to get what they wanted: closure for her, preserving his dad's legacy for him.

Finally finding voice, he cleared his throat. 'Thanks, Babs, I'll have the transfer papers drawn up immediately.'

She nodded, picked up her designer bag, and barged out

of the room, leaving the board members watching him carefully.

What did they expect? For him to cartwheel across the highly polished conference table? He might've been tempted, if not for the fact he had serious business to conduct after this meeting.

Business far more important than *Qu Publishing*.

Business of the heart.

Chapter Twenty-Four

Liza hadn't expected Wade to show up again so soon after their morning outing.

When she'd dropped him at the office earlier he'd been withdrawn, and while he'd mustered a genuine goodbye for Cindy he'd shot her the oddest look: like he was disappointed in her.

She knew why. She'd been uncomfortable discussing her parents and how she supported Cindy, and he'd picked up on her evasiveness. If he only knew how far she'd come in letting him spend time with Cindy today, and lowering her guard in front of him. That had been a big step for her. Huge. But she couldn't blab all her deep, dark secrets at once. She had to take this slow.

To find him waiting for her in the living room while Shar and Cindy had a late supper on the back porch made her incredibly happy that he couldn't bear to be away from her for more than half a day. Though her cautious side couldn't be ignored and she wondered if his impromptu visit heralded bad news.

'Would you like a drink?'

He shook his head. 'No thanks, I'd rather talk.'

'Okay.'

She perched next to him on the sofa, wondering if he noticed the threadbare patches on the shabby chintz. Those patches made her angry. She'd scrimped and saved, hoarding every cent away for Cindy's future, going without stuff like new furniture because she didn't deem it as important as having a failsafe should anything happen to her.

Instead, something had happened to her money and while the advance and royalties would help, the thought of being conned out of her sizeable savings made her stomach gripe.

'Are you all right?'

'Yeah, why?' She met his gaze, knowing he was far too astute not to notice her jumpiness.

'You seem distracted.'

She tapped her temple. 'I'm making a mental to-do list for tomorrow and it's a doozy.'

He nodded, his grave expression indicating he didn't buy her excuse for a second. 'I've got news.'

Trepidation made her freeze as various scenarios, each of them worse than the last, filtered through her brain. Pre-orders had fallen through. Bookstores had reneged on stocking her biography. Online advertisers had pulled their backing. Early reviews had been appalling.

Quelling her nerves with effort, she said, 'What's the news?'

He eyeballed her and she didn't like the wariness she glimpsed.

'With *Qu Publishing* in the black, I'm going back to London.'

The blood drained from her head and spots danced before Liza's eyes before she blinked, inhaled, steadied.

'My business is there and I've been away long enough.'

'Of course,' she said, grateful her tone remained neutral and modulated, when she felt like screaming.

'I want you to come with me.' He took her hand, rubbed its iciness between his. 'You and Cindy.'

Shock tore through every preconception Liza had ever had about this guy. He was returning to his life and he wanted her and Cindy to be a part of it?

If she didn't love him before, she sure as hell did now.

Love?

Uh-oh. A fine time to realise she loved Wade when she was on the verge of hyperventilating, collapsing, or both.

What could she say?

A thousand responses sprang to her lips, none of them appropriate. She couldn't uproot Cindy. Couldn't lose Shar. Couldn't do any of this without the stability she'd worked so damn hard to maintain.

It had been her priority when her folks, particularly her mum, left. Trying to maintain normality. Pretend everything was okay. That the two of them would be fine.

To tear that all away from Cindy on a whim to follow her heart?

She couldn't do it.

Had Wade really thought this through? Had he considered what it would be like living with her and her sister? His place would need to be remodelled and that was only one of the many changes he'd have to cope with.

What if he grew tired of it? What if he couldn't handle having Cindy full time? What if Cindy grew to love him as much as she did and then he ended it? The emotional fallout from something so major would definitely have a detrimental effect on Cindy physically.

No, one Lithgow sister having her heart broken was

enough. She'd vowed to protect Cindy and, sadly, that meant giving up her one shot at happiness.

'Your silence is scaring me,' he said, continuing to chafe her hand in his, but no amount of rubbing could stem the iciness trickling through her veins and chilling every extremity.

'I think you're incredible for asking us to come with you, Wade, but we can't.'

His hands stilled. 'Can't or won't?'

'Both,' she said, wondering if that was the first impulsively honest thing she'd ever told him.

She'd spent a decade carefully weighing her words, saying the right thing, doing the right thing, yet now, when it would pay to be circumspect, a plethora of words bubbled up from deep within and threatened to spill out.

'The fact you care enough to include Cindy in your offer means more to me than you'll ever know, but I can't uproot her.'

She gestured to the backyard where the sound of voices and laughter drifted inside. 'She's comfortable here, she's safe. It's the only home she's ever known and I can't move her halfway across the world.'

He willed her to look at him, his gaze boring into her, but she determinedly stared at their joined hands.

'She'll have the best of carers and medical professionals. I can afford it—'

'No.' The vehement refusal sounded like a gunshot. Short. Sharp. Ominous. 'I've always taken care of her and I'll continue to do so.'

He released her hand and eased away as if she'd slapped him. 'Is it so hard to accept help? Or are you too used to playing the martyr you'd do anything to continue the role?

And shouldn't Cindy get a say in this? In how she wants to live her life?'

His harsh accusation hung in the growing silence while a lump of hurt and anger and regret welled in her chest until she could hardly breathe.

He swiped a hand across his face. 'Sorry, that was way out of line. But you need to realise you have a life too—'

'My life is here, right where I want to be,' she said, finally raising her eyes to meet his, seeing the precise second he registered her bleakness. 'Cindy is all I have and I'm not going to abandon her.'

'But you won't be.' He tried to reach for her and she wriggled back. 'You're not your folks, Liza, you're so much better than them. But the strain of bearing a constant load will eventually tell. It's not healthy shouldering everything by yourself.'

He tapped his chest. 'Let me in. I'll be here for you. Always.'

That sounded awfully like forever to Liza and it only added to her grief. She'd be walking away from the best man she'd ever met.

But she didn't hesitate, not for a second. Wade was right about one thing. She wasn't her folks and there was nothing he could do or say that would make her put her needs ahead of her sister's.

She shook her head, unable to stop the tears spilling from her eyes. 'I can't. Sorry.'

And then she ran. Ran from the house, ran from the man she loved, ran from a bright future. Ran until her lungs seized and her legs buckled. Even then, she kept pushing, jogging four blocks before she registered the car cruising beside her.

When she finally couldn't take another step from sheer

exhaustion, she stopped, braced her hands on her thighs, and bent over to inhale lungfuls of air. It didn't ease the pain tightening her chest in a vice.

She ignored the car idling on the kerb, ignored the electronic glide of a window sliding down.

'Get in,' Wade said. 'I'll take you home.'

Liza shook her head, willing the strength to return to her legs so she could make another dash for it. She needed to escape Wade and his kindness, not be confined in his car.

'I'm not leaving until you do.'

She lifted her head, mustering a glare that fell short considering sweat dripped in her eyes and her hair stuck to her forehead in lank strands.

Then she glimpsed the devastation clouding his eyes and something inside her broke.

How could she treat this amazingly beautiful man so badly?

He didn't deserve this. He deserved a friendly parting, a thank you for giving her a job and a lifeline at a time she needed it most.

So she sucked in her bruised pride and hobbled toward the car, feeling as if a baseball bat had battered her as she sank onto the plush leather seat.

He didn't speak, intuitive to her needs until the very end, and it only served to increase her respect, love, and gratitude.

When Wade pulled up outside her house, she mustered what was left of her minimal dignity.

'Thanks for everything.' Her breath hitched and she continued on a sob. 'I'll never forget you.'

She fumbled with the door handle, tumbled out of the car, and bolted without looking back.

This time, he didn't come after her.

Chapter Twenty-Five

Wade packed on autopilot. Suits in bags, shirts in the case, shoes stuffed in the sides, the rest flung over the top.

He liked the mindless, methodical job. It kept his hands busy. A good distraction, because otherwise he'd be likely to thump something.

Punching a hole in the wall of his penthouse wouldn't be a good idea at this point, as he didn't have time to organise plasterers to fix it. He wanted to leave ASAP. The sooner the better. There was nothing left for him here anymore. He'd done what he'd set out to do. Save *Qu Publishing*. Preserve his father's legacy. Make some amends for ruining their relationship.

Everything else that had happened? A blip on the radar, soon forgotten when he returned to London.

Until he made the fatal mistake of glancing at the bed and it all came flooding back.

Liza on top of him, pinning his wrists overhead, her hair draping his chest.

Liza beneath him, arching upward, writhing in pleasure.

Liza snuggled in the circle of his arms, her hand splayed on his chest, over his heart, keeping it safe.

Or so he'd thought.

With a groan, he abandoned his packing and sank onto the bed, dropped his head in his hands, and acknowledged the pain.

He'd deliberately closed off after he'd left her house, and had driven to his penthouse in a fog of numbness. It had worked for him before, when he'd made the decision to leave the family business and strike out on his own in London.

He remembered his dad's disappointment, his surprise, and the only way Wade had dealt with it back then was to erect emotional barriers and get on with the job. It served him well, compartmentalising his life and his emotions, forgoing one for the sake of the other.

But look how that had turned out, with his dad having a heart condition he knew nothing about and Wade distancing himself when he could've made the most of every moment.

Maybe his coping mechanism wasn't so great after all?

Maybe he'd be better off confronting his demons than running from them?

Maybe he should lower the emotional barriers he'd raised to protect himself and take a chance on trusting someone again?

Because that's what hurt him the most with his dad: that their breakdown in trust had affected how he interacted with everyone, from his colleagues to his dates. He didn't allow anyone to get close for fear of being let down, the way he'd felt when his dad had put Babs first at the expense of their relationship.

He'd never understood how Quentin could tolerate their strained relationship for that woman.

Until now.

Love did strange things to a guy and if his dad had been half as smitten with Babs as Wade was with Liza, he could justify his behaviour. It didn't make accepting their lost years any easier or the lack of trust he'd instilled in his dad because of his withdrawal, both physical and emotional, but it went some way to easing the guilt.

He wondered how different his life would be if he didn't run this time.

A thousand scenarios flashed through his head, the main one centred on Liza and him, together. He thought he'd made her an offer too good to refuse, a magnanimous gesture including her sister. But the more he thought about it, the more he realised how selfish he'd been.

Had he really expected her to pack up, leave her support network, and move halfway around the world to fit in with his life?

At no stage had he contemplated staying in Melbourne. It had been a given he'd return to London and expected her to make all the sacrifices. He should've known she'd never agree.

Maybe that was why he'd done it?

Issued an offer he knew she could never accept?

The thought rattled him. He'd never been emotionally involved with a woman, had kept his dalliances emotion free. The way he saw it, inviting her to live with him had been a huge step forward.

But what if it wasn't forward enough?

He'd treated his dad the same way, not willing to see

two sides of their story, intent on believing what he wanted to believe. It had ruined their relationship and driven an irrevocable wedge between them.

It irked, how he'd never have a second chance with his dad. But it wasn't too late to make amends with Liza...

Wade leapt from the bed and headed to the living room in search of his phone. He needed to put some feelers out, set some plans in motion, before he took the chance of his lifetime.

This time, he wouldn't screw up.

Chapter Twenty-Six

Liza cherished movie nights with Cindy. She loved curling up on the couch, a massive bowl of popcorn and a packet of chocolate cookies between them, laughing uproariously at their favourite comedies they rewatched countless times.

But tonight, not even the funniest animated ogre could dredge up a chuckle. Cindy had picked up on her mood, barely making a dent in the popcorn when she usually devoured the lot.

'Are you sad because Wade left?'

Reluctant to discuss this with Cindy because she didn't want to stress her out unnecessarily, Liza dragged her gaze from the TV screen and forced a smile for her sister, knowing she'd have to give Cindy some semblance of the truth for her to drop the topic.

'Yeah, I'll miss him.'

A tiny frown marred Cindy's brow. 'Where is he going?'

'London.'

'Wow.' Cindy's eyes widened to huge blue orbs. 'Lucky guy. London's an amazing city. Wish we could go.'

Cindy crammed another fistful of popcorn into her mouth, chewed, before continuing. 'Maybe we could visit Wade there?'

Stunned, Liza stared at Cindy. She'd never heard her sister articulate any great desire to travel. The furthest they'd been was Sydney when Jimmy had been up for a mega award, and Liza had spent the entire time torn between caring for Cindy and ensuring she presented the perfect WAG front when on Jimmy's arm.

It had been exhausting, and after that weekend she preferred to spend time with Cindy at home, while keeping her travels for WAG duties separate.

Not that they'd been able to afford travel. She'd been so busy saving every cent for the future she'd never contemplated wasting money on an overseas trip.

'Wade's a good guy. He likes you.' Cindy smirked. 'I think you like him too.'

Liza sighed. If only it was as simple as that.

'London's a long way away, sweetie—'

'That's what planes are for, dummy.' Cindy elbowed her. 'You should buy tickets. We should go.'

Reeling from Cindy's suggestion, Liza nudged the popcorn bowl closer and gestured at the TV, grateful when Cindy became absorbed in the movie again.

She needed to think. Not that she'd contemplate flying to London for a vacation, not after she'd worked so hard to replace part of her nest egg for Cindy, but hearing Cindy's request opened her eyes in a way she'd never anticipated.

Had she been so focused on providing financial security she'd lost sight of the bigger picture? That in an effort to protect her sister she'd actually been stifling her?

Wade had accused her of not giving Cindy a choice when he'd made his offer and it irked at the time because deep down she knew she was overprotective when it came to her sister. She'd justified it for years because Cindy had been nine when Liza became her legal guardian and she'd had to make the tough decisions.

Everything she'd done had been for Cindy but in focussing on making life easier for her sister, had she robbed Cindy of a chance to build resilience? To embrace independence? To learn from her mistakes?

Guilt blossomed in her chest and she absent-mindedly rubbed it, wishing she could ease the continual ache in her heart. But since Wade had driven away last night, the pain had lingered, intensified, until she accepted it as a permanent fixture. Niggling, annoying, there until she got over him. Whenever that was.

Cindy laughed at the ogre's antics while Liza contemplated the disservice she'd been doing her sister. All these years she'd assumed Cindy had been content. But by her excitement in proposing a London trip, maybe Cindy craved adventure? Maybe she felt as if she was missing out somehow?

In building a secure life, had Liza transferred her fear of abandonment onto Cindy, ensuring her sister felt cloistered rather than free to grow?

But Liza couldn't move to London with Wade. It wasn't feasible or practical. Then again, hadn't she lived a practical life the last decade? Faking smiles for the cameras, dressed in uncomfortable designer gear for events, pretending to like her date when she couldn't wait to get home at the end of a long awards night.

She'd built her entire reputation on a mirage, on a woman who didn't exist, to the point she hardly knew the real her anymore.

Yet Wade had taken a chance on her anyway.

He'd trusted her enough, loved her enough, to offer her a new life and had included her sister in it.

What kind of guy did that?

An honourable, understanding, caring guy. A guy who wasn't afraid of taking chances. Who wasn't afraid of letting people into his life.

Liza didn't like risks. Losing her folks and losing her savings had ensured that. And if she couldn't take risks with her life, no way would she take risks with Cindy's.

Which brought her right back to the beginning of her dilemma.

She loved Wade. The only guy she'd ever truly loved. But she'd let him go because she was too scared to take a risk, too scared he'd eventually walk away from her.

'You're missing the best bit,' Cindy said, grabbing a biscuit and offering her the last one in the pack.

'It's all yours,' Liza said, draping a hand across her sister's shoulder and squeezing tight.

Everything she did was for this incredible girl by her side, and she'd have to keep remembering that over the next few months while her shattered heart took an eternity to mend.

Liza would like nothing better than to take a chance on Wade.

But as Cindy snuggled into her side, Liza knew some risks were too big to take.

Chapter Twenty-Seven

Wade had never been a gambler.

He preferred to weigh the pros and cons of any decision carefully, consider all the options, before choosing the most logical answer, the most feasible outcome.

All that sensible bull had gone out of the window when he'd taken the biggest gamble of his life and asked Liza to meet him here.

He had no idea if she'd show.

She hadn't answered his call so he'd left a message about meeting him here. Her terse response an hour later didn't bode well.

> Will think about it

He didn't want to bug her so hadn't responded to her text, but he'd turned up at the hotel bar where they'd first met anyway, hoping she'd take a chance.

If there was one thing he was sure of in this mess, it was her love.

She hadn't said the words. He hadn't either, considering she'd been too busy busting his balls and throwing his offer back in his face. But he'd seen it in her eyes: the adoration, the tenderness, the agony at the thought of never being together.

He felt the same way, processing a gamut of emotions ranging from devastation to optimism. No more. He might be trusting gut instinct right now but he'd applied logic to make it happen.

Every contingency plan had been put into place.

Now all he needed was for Liza to say yes.

He nursed his whiskey, swirling it around, instantly transported back to the night they'd met, the night they'd shared a drink here, the night that had set him down this rocky road.

For a guy who never let emotions get in the way of anything, he'd sure botched this, big time.

He took a swig of his drink and glanced at his watch. Nine p.m. and Liza was a no-show. He'd give her ten minutes and then he was out of here.

As pain lanced his heart, he thought, *Who are you trying to kid?*

He'd probably end up sitting here all night if there was the remotest possibility she'd walk in the door.

As if his wish had been granted, he saw Liza enter, lock eyes with him, and pause. She looked stunning, from the top of her glossy blonde hair piled in a loose up-do to her shimmery turquoise dress to her sparkly silver-sequinned sandals. Guys in the bar gawked and he wanted to flatten them all.

He stood as she made her way toward him, torn between wanting to vault tables to get to her and sit on his hands to stop from grabbing her the moment she got within reach. The nearer she got, the harder his gut twisted until he could barely stand.

'Hey.' She hesitated when she reached him, then kissed him on the cheek before taking a seat opposite.

'Thanks for coming.' He sounded like a doofus but he sat, relieved she made it. 'I didn't think you'd show.'

She held her thumb and forefinger an inch apart. 'I was this close to not coming.'

'Why the change of heart?'

She glanced away, gnawing on her bottom lip, before reluctantly meeting his gaze. 'Because you deserved better than the way I treated you the last time we parted.'

'Fair enough.'

He liked that about her, her bluntness. She might not have been completely honest with him the last few months, but her ability to call a spade a spade when it counted meant a lot. He hoped she'd continue in that vein for the rest of the evening, because he'd settle for nothing less than the truth.

'Drink?'

'Anything but a martini,' she said, managing a wan smile.

'Sure? Because I like what happens when you drink martinis.'

The sparkle in her eyes gave him hope. 'Soda and lemon for now.'

'Spoilsport,' he said, placing the order with a nearby waiter before swivelling back to face her.

'I was going to call you,' she said, her hands twisting in her lap before she slid them under her handbag. 'I wanted to apologise for the craziness after you asked me to move to London.'

'Not necessary—'

'Yes, it is.'

The waiter deposited her soda on the table and she grabbed it and downed half the glass before continuing.

'You caught me completely off guard. I mean, I knew you'd be heading back eventually, but I didn't expect it to be so soon, and then you asked me to come along with Cindy in tow and I flipped out.'

'I noticed.'

She matched his wry smile. 'I've never had anyone care about me that much to include Cindy in our plans.'

Her fingertips fluttered over her heart. 'It touched me right here and I didn't know how to articulate half of what I was feeling.'

That made two of them. He'd become an expert at bottling up true feelings, preferring not to rock the boat, seeking other outlets for his frustration rather than attacking the root of the problem.

If only he'd confronted his dad sooner, had a talk man to man, rather than skulking off to London with his bitterness, the last few years would've been completely different.

'So I want to say thanks, Wade. Your offer means more to me than you'll ever know.'

'But?'

Her gaze dropped to her fiddling hands. 'But ultimately my decision stands. I can't move to London to be with you.'

'Thought so,' he said, stifling a chuckle at her confused frown at his chipper tone. 'Which is why I'm changing the parameters of the offer.'

Her frown deepened. 'I don't understand.'

'I'm staying in Melbourne.'

Speechless, she gaped at him until he placed a fingertip beneath her chin and closed her mouth.

The PLAYER

'I've installed my deputy as the new CEO in my London office. He'll run the place and answer to me.'

He sat back and rested an arm across the back of his chair, bringing his hand within tantalising touching distance of her bare shoulder. 'I'm taking over the reins of *Qu Publishing*. Finishing what my father started all those years ago. It's what he would've wanted.'

Another revelation he'd had while instigating steps to remain in Melbourne, making a business choice he should've years earlier. An invisible weight had lifted from his shoulders, the guilt he'd harboured in relation to the gap between him and his dad evaporating once he'd made the decision to run the company.

He knew it was what his dad would've wanted. How many times had they discussed it, before Wade had got sick of Babs and her influence over his father and had moved to London? Many times, and he'd seen his dad's shattered expression the day he'd told him of his plans to relocate and start a new business.

It had haunted him and, while they'd never broached the subject again during their brief catch-ups over the years, he'd sensed his dad's disappointment.

Yeah, the decision to stay in Melbourne was the correct one.

Now he had to convince Liza of that.

'My offer still stands. Move in with me. Give our relationship a chance.' He touched her shoulder, sliding his hand along the back of her neck and resting it there. 'I love you, Liza, and from a guy who's never said those three little words before, trust me, it's a big call.'

Tears shimmered in her eyes and he scooted closer, swiping away a few that trickled down her cheeks.

'A resounding yes would be great right about now,' he said, cuddling her into his side.

Her silence unnerved him but he waited. He'd waited this long to meet the love of his life, what were a few more minutes?

She sniffled and dabbed under her eyes before easing away to look him in the eye.

'But Cindy—'

'The parameters of my offer have changed somewhat.' He cupped her chin. 'I'm asking you to move in with me. Just you.'

Her eyes widened and she started to shake her head but his grip tightened.

'I'm blown away by your dedication to your sister, truly I am. I've never met such a self-sacrificing person. But I think you're using Cindy as a crutch, hiding behind her, afraid to take chances.'

His thumb brushed her lower lip. 'Ultimately, sweetheart? That's not going to help either of you.'

Anger flashed in her eyes before she wrenched away. 'Who the hell do you think you are, telling me what I feel and how I'm running my life?'

'I'm the guy who loves you, the guy who'll do anything to make you happy.' He laid a hand on her knee, surprised and grateful when she didn't shrug him off. 'If you'll let me.'

She glared at him a moment longer before she visibly deflated. Her shoulders sagged and her head drooped, and he moved in quickly to support her with an arm around her waist.

'Cindy wants to go to London.' She spoke so softly Wade had to lean closer to hear. 'It made me realise that maybe I've cosseted her too much.'

She shook her head and a few tendrils tumbled around

her face. 'I've spent most of my life trying to protect her but now I'm wondering...'

When she didn't speak, Wade said, 'What?'

She dragged in a breath and blew it out. 'I'm wondering if I did more harm than good, sheltering her the way I have.'

'You love her. It's natural you'd want to protect her after your folks ran out.'

'It's more than that.'

She glanced at him, her forlorn expression slugging him in the guts. It took every ounce of his will power not to bundle her into his arms.

'I think I used her. I liked having her dependent on me, because that way she couldn't abandon me.'

As her folks did. Liza didn't have to say it, it was written all over her face: her fear of being alone.

'Is that why you're not doing cartwheels over my offer now? Because you think ultimately I'll abandon you too?'

She appeared shocked at his perceptiveness.

'I won't, you know.' He grabbed her hand and placed it against his heart, beating madly for her, only her. 'I don't let people into my heart easily. I've never had a long-term relationship. It took me a while to trust you. I even pushed away my dad through sheer narrow-mindedness. But once I give it, it's all yours.'

He added, 'Forever.'

Her tremulous smile made him hope. 'You're incredible, the most amazing guy I've ever met, but I've never depended on anyone before. I'll be no good at it. I'll screw up and you'll get sick of me and then—'

'Say it.'

'Then you'll leave me,' she said, so softly his heart turned over beneath her palm.

'There are no guarantees in life, but how about this? I

promise to love you and cherish you and look after you to the best of my ability. How's that?'

'Pretty damn wonderful.' She beamed and he could've sworn the bar lit up like a bright summer's day.

'So no more secrets, okay?'

Her face fell. 'Then in the event of full disclosure, I need to tell you what happened in your office that first day.'

He'd been curious but hadn't wanted to push for answers. With a little luck he'd have plenty of time for that: like the rest of their lives.

'Why I embraced the WAG lifestyle and put up with being arm candy for Henri when we weren't in a real relationship?' She grimaced. 'I did it for the money. We had a signed agreement. I was building a sizeable nest egg for Cindy's future in case anything ever happened to me.'

Her abandonment issues ran deep. Considering what she'd been through with her folks, he understood.

'The night we met, when I said I was embarking on a new life and wanted to celebrate? I was stoked to be putting my old life behind me. It had taken its toll and I was tired of faking it for everyone.'

Her fingers clenched, creasing the cotton of his shirt. 'My investments were maturing the next day and I had grand plans to tie up some of it in a guaranteed fund for Cindy in case of my death, and use the rest to modernise our place and buy her the best equipment. With that kind of monetary security, it was the beginning of a new life for me. I could finally pursue a career in marketing, my dream, and put the past behind me.'

A few pieces of the puzzle shifted and he had a fair idea what she was going to say. She would've never agreed to the publishing contract after vehemently refusing it unless she needed the money. Which meant someone had taken advantage of her.

'What happened to your investment?'

Her eyes darkened to indigo, filled with pain. 'My financial adviser absconded with the lot. Scammed millions in client funds.'

He swore.

'The police are investigating leads but the likelihood of recovering my cash are slim.'

'That's why you did an about-face with the publishing deal.'

She nodded. 'I needed that money as a safeguard for Cindy. It was the only way.'

He hesitated, glad they were talking things through but needing to know all of it, however unpleasant.

'I've seen how much you love Cindy, so you're not ashamed of her.' He grimaced. 'Sorry for saying that. So why did you really leave her out of your biography?'

'I always thought it was fear of her spasticity worsening and resulting in permanent deformities if her emotions careened out of control with the probable media circus.'

She smoothed his shirt and let her hand fall, only to clasp his and squeeze. 'In reality? I think it's because I'm overprotective to the point of stifling. I've tried so hard to make up for our parents' shortfalls I've gone the other way and become smothering. I didn't want Cindy exposed to any judgemental media, which can still happen to disabled people even in this enlightened day, so I cut her out of the story.'

'Did you ever stop to think how she'd feel if she knew that? Because she told me she loves reading and that means she'll read your biography and wonder why you omitted her.'

Her brows arched in horror. 'I was doing it to protect her—'

'I know, sweetheart, I know.' Maybe he needed to quit while he was ahead. 'You still haven't answered my original question.'

The corners of her mouth curved up and he had his answer before she spoke.

'I'll have to chat with Shar and see if she can become a permanent live-in carer. And I'll need a raise to cover it. Plus I still want to spend as much time as possible with Cindy.'

'Anything else?'

'Just this.'

She surged against him, grabbed his lapels, dragged him closer, and kissed him.

The teasing wolf whistles of nearby patrons faded as her lips moved against his and he wished he'd had the foresight to book a suite.

When she finally broke the kiss, he grinned. 'That's a yes, then?'

'You bet.'

She cupped his face and stared unwaveringly into his eyes. 'And I love you too. How did I get so lucky?'

'*We* got lucky.'

He kissed her again to prove it.

Epilogue

'Wow, check out the view.'

Cindy pressed her face against the glass pod of the London Eye, captivated by the incredible view of the city below them.

'Amazing, huh?' Liza slung an arm around Cindy's shoulders and squeezed, her heart full to bursting.

Seeing her sister's wonder as they visited every popular tourist site—the Tower of London, Buckingham Palace, St. Paul's Cathedral, Kew Gardens, Westminster Abbey—sharing in Cindy's joyful exuberance, made for precious memories.

'Sure is.' Cindy tore her awestruck gaze away from the view long enough to glance at Wade. 'Thanks for allowing me to tag along, Wade. You're the best.'

'No worries, kiddo.' He dropped a kiss on the top of Cindy's head and Liza's heart flip-flopped. Could she love this guy any more than she already did?

He didn't treat Cindy as an adjunct to their relationship, he included her in it, and his affection for her sister was something Liza was thankful for every day.

'Hey, what about me?'

Liza's fake pout made Cindy roll her eyes. 'You were the best, until you left me out of your book.'

Liza winced. 'We've talked about this and you know why I did it.'

'Yeah, yeah, you were being a helicopter sister, hovering over me, I get it.' Cindy glanced at Wade and winked. 'How you put up with her neuroses, I'll never know.'

Wade laughed and held up his hands. 'I'm staying out of this sisterly battle, because I happen to think you're both the coolest women on the planet.'

Cindy leaned in close to Liza and murmured, 'Suck up,' loud enough for Wade to hear, and they laughed.

'I can see you two making those obnoxious lovey-dovey eyes at each other, so go over there.' Cindy made a shooing motion. 'And leave me to savour this incredible view in peace.'

'Damn, you're bossy,' Liza said, leaning down to give Cindy a hug before moving to the other side of the pod with Wade.

When he opened his arms she happily moved into his embrace, and brushed a soft kiss against his lips.

'You're incredible, you know that?'

He smiled and nodded at Cindy. 'So I've been told by your incredibly astute sister.'

'Well, I'm telling you again.' Liza snuggled tighter, content in the knowledge there was no better place to be than Wade's arms. 'The way you put this trip together, checked out disabled facilities at all the places we've visited, did a renovation on your apartment for Cindy to stay. Not to mention pulling together the digital companion novel to my biography highlighting cerebral palsy and the needs of carers to raise awareness...'

The PLAYER

She stood on tiptoe and whispered in his ear. 'Remember how I was scared you'd leave me one day? Forget it, babe, because I'm going to be glued to your side for life.'

He laughed and hugged her tight. 'Make that a promise and you've got yourself a deal.'

Liza's WAG Wow tips

A note from the author.
In the original version of this book, I had Liza's style tips placed at the start of every chapter from her point of view as a bit of light-hearted fun.
But I decided it might distract readers from the story, hence I've collated them all together here.
Enjoy!

Liza hopes you enjoy her WAG WOW tips.

While she may have left her WAG days behind, she regularly indulges in the following recommendations.

Though she's rarely alone to indulge in some of the tips mentioned here these days, what with Wade to keep her company...

LIZA'S STYLE TIPS FOR WAG WOW

The Shape

Liza's WAG Wow tips

The key to WAG wow is making the most of what you have.

Learn how to show off your best assets and how to visually change the body parts you'd rather hide.

Always dress to suit your shape.

PEAR

a) Wear dark colours on the lower half of your body.

b) A-line skirts that skim the hips and butt are flattering.

c) Accessorise with scarves, necklaces, and earrings to draw attention to the upper half of your body.

d) Avoid light coloured pants or anything too tight on your bottom half.

BUSTY

a) Go for flattering necklines with tops and dresses: turtle necks, shirt collars, boat necks, V necks.

b) Go for high-sitting necklaces as they draw the gaze up.

c) Avoid baggy tops with no shape as they can make you look heavier and avoid anything too tight across the chest.

SHORT

a) Dresses ending above the knee are best.

b) Wear fitted tops and trousers (straight or bootleg).

c) Avoid cropped length pants as they make legs look shorter.

TALL

a) Wear different colours top and bottom to break up the illusion of length.

b) Wear horizontal stripes.

c) Wear well-fitted layers that skim the body.

d) Adding a wide belt can help create a nice shape.

e) Avoid wearing pants that are the incorrect length.

Remember, the key to appearing confident in the clothes you wear is to be comfortable.

Liza's WAG Wow tips

How many times have we seen women tugging up their strapless bodices or tugging down their micro-minis? It's not a good look.

When you strut into a room, being confident in your body and the look you've created is half the battle!

THE CLASSICS

You don't need money to create a WAG wow look. Designer bargains, vintage chic, and good accessories can create an outfit that will have the paparazzi snap-happy.

To create a timeless, elegant look consistently, it's worthwhile investing in a few classic pieces, the items in any WAG's wardrobe that will always be in style.

Little black dress. *A staple, so buy several: different lengths, necklines, fitted. The classic LBD is a lifesaver and can be combined with various jacket/shoe combinations to give the illusion of many different looks.*

Jacket. *Make sure it's expensive and tailored. It will last forever.*

Heels. *Black patent leather stilettos will never go out of style.*

Sunglasses. *Brand names are classy. Enlist the help of an honest shop assistant to ensure the shape/size suits your face.*

Boots. *Black and brown leather boots can be worn with anything and everything. High heels and flats in both recommended.*

Striped top. *Black and white stripes are a staple. Dress up or down.*

Ballet flats. *Perfect to pop into your bag to use at the end of a long day at the polo or a long night dancing.*

Liza's WAG Wow tips

Pants. *Tailored black and beige will go with almost anything. Wide leg is elegant. Bootleg flattering.*

Belt. *Thin, black leather. Classic.*

Cardigan. *Cream cashmere, can't go wrong.*

Clutch. *Smaller than a handbag yet makes a bigger statement.*

Handbag. *Must carry everything but bigger isn't always better. Co-ordinate handbag to your outfit and shoes. Choose neutral colours: black, tan, brown. Mid-size with handles and shoulder strap best.*

Jeans. *Discover which style suits you best and stick with it. But for maximum WAG wow, have denim in various cuts: skinny, bootleg, boyfriend, etc.*

Trench-coat. *Double-breasted, belted, beige. Classic.*

Watch. *For timeless elegance, invest in an expensive watch. People notice.*

Bling. *Take the 'less is best' approach. Diamond stud earrings. Thin white gold necklace. Unless your sports star partner wins the championship for his team, then get him to buy you a diamond mine and then some.*

THE LASHES

The eyes have it. Whether attending a grand final at a stadium packed with one hundred thousand people, a glamorous nightclub opening, or a BBQ with the team and their partners, bold eyes make a statement.

1) Prep with a hydrating cream.

2) Apply foundation over your lids.

3) Draw the perfect line with pencil, then trace with liquid eyeliner.

4) Apply shadow of choice. Go for sparkle at night.

5) Finish with lashings of mascara.

If you need a little help in the lash department extensions are the way to go. Individual fake lashes are pasted to your own, giving you a lush look that turns heads.

A full set of extensions takes about an hour. They last 3-6 weeks and will require refills at this time. Refills take 30 minutes.

If you prefer 'au natural' the key to luscious lashes is prepping with a good serum. Many cosmetic companies have them.

To open up the eye in preparation for mascara, eyelash curlers are essential. Best to heat them up slightly before applying pressure to the lashes for thirty-seconds.

For more dramatic impact with mascara, wiggle the wand from side to side as you apply, ensuring good coverage at the base of the lashes. It's the density and darkness of mascara at the roots that give the illusion of length.

And always, always, opt for waterproof. (You never know when your sport star 'other half' may shoot the winning hoop to win the national championship or kick the goal to break a nil-all draw.)

For real wow factor with mascara, the darker the better. Black is best unless you have a very fair complexion, in which case brown is better. Similarly with eyeliner. Stick to black at night and softer, smudged brown during the day.

For eyeshadow shades, stick to neutrals or soft pinks. Let your lashes do the talking!

THE LIPS

For the height of sophistication and glam WOW, the perfect pout is where it's at. Having a palette of colours for various looks is essential. Co-ordinate colour with outfits.

Liza's WAG Wow tips

Go bold with fire engine red for an awards ceremony or pastel pink for the season opener.

Keep lips soft so that means no lip liner!

For a fabulous femme fatale pout, preparation is key.

1) Gently exfoliate lips with a soft-bristled toothbrush.

2) Moisturise with a specialised lip balm.

3) Use a lip-fix cream which prevents colour bleeding.

4) Apply lipstick once. Blot with tissue. Re-apply.

For a subtle look, pat lipstick on with a fingertip.

For bold lips, apply with a lip brush. Blot. Reapply.

If you want a plump pout without the injections, try lipsticks with inbuilt 'fillers'.

These innovative ingredients are proven to increase lip volume by forty percent. Amazing!

They also hydrate and restore collagen over time.

A dab of gloss in the middle of the lower lip is a subtle touch that adds real WOW!

THE HAIR

For ultra-glam events like the MVP Awards (and especially if your guy is favoured to win the Most Valuable Player award) it pays to indulge in a trip to a hair salon. Even if you don't go for a fancy up-do, blow-out sleek hair is always in vogue.

For maximum DIY WAG wow, try the loose knot. It's sophisticated and relaxed and sexy all at the same time, the perfect do if you're aiming for understated elegance.

Here's how you do it:

Wash your hair.

Add a volumising mousse to damp hair.

Blow dry hair from the ends to the roots to create more volume.

Liza's WAG Wow tips

Use a comb to tease the crown.
Using fingers, gather hair in a low ponytail.
Secure with a band.
Fix into a loose bun with pins and let strands fall.
Finish with a light spritz of hairspray to secure.

If you're dying to try a different look but don't have the length required, hair extensions are an option. But make sure they blend with your colour and get an expert to do them.

You don't want a clump of hair dislodging at an inopportune moment (like when the TV cameras are panning to you when your guy wins that MVP award!

THE CITY

Depending how famous the sportsman, WAGs get to travel, but home is where the heart is. Here are my tips for getting to know beautiful Melbourne.

1. Acland Street, St. Kilda. *An iconic street lined with cake and pastry shops. Dare you to stop at trying one! And on Sundays, check out the market on the nearby Esplanade.*

2. Lygon Street, Carlton. *The Little Italy of Melbourne, a street lined with fabulous restaurants and cafés. Try the thin-crusted pizzas and the espressos. You won't be able to walk past the gelato outlets without succumbing!*

3. Victoria Street, Richmond. *If you love Vietnamese food this street is for you. Choose from the many restaurants filled with fragrant steam from soups and sizzling dishes. And if you love to shop, check out nearby Bridge Road with its many brand outlets. Bargains galore.*

4. Southbank. *Stroll along the Yarra River and try to*

decide which fabulous café you'll dine in. Or check out the funky shops.

5. Docklands. *If you like to eat by the water's edge, this area is for you. Many hip restaurants.*

6. Dandenong Ranges. *The mountain range just over an hour from the city, where you'll find many quaint B&Bs, craft shops, and cafés to explore. Also home to the iconic Puffing Billy steam train, which takes you on a leisurely ride through the lush forest.*

7. Phillip Island. *If you like cute animals and the beach, you'll love this place. Stroll the surf beach and, at night, check out the fairy penguins.*

8. Federation Square. *In the heart of the city, Fed Square is home to restaurants, cafés, and cultural displays.*

9. MCG. *WAGs in all sports codes have usually visited the Melbourne Cricket Ground at some stage. Home of the AFL Grand Final, watched by millions around the world. A visit to the sports museum here is worth it.*

10. Little Bourke Street. *In the heart of the city, Chinatown in Melbourne, lined with fabulous Chinese restaurants. Hard to choose!*

11. Chapel Street, South Yarra. *About 10 minutes from the city, you'll find an eclectic mix of boutiques, restaurants, and cafés here. Worth strolling to people-watch alone.*

12. Queen Victoria Market. *Food and fashion bargains, with everything in between. A fun way to pass a few hours.*

13. Daylesford. *This quaint town is in the heart of 'Spa Country'. The amazing baths at neighbouring town Hepburn Springs are a must visit. The area is home to gourmet food and artists. Visit the Convent Gallery for a combination of both.*

14. Brunswick Street, Fitzroy. *An eclectic mix of cafés, boutiques, & clubs.*

THE BIG CHILL

Melbourne is renowned for its chilly winters but that doesn't mean WAGs need to lose their wow. Here's how to beat the big chill:

1. Even though your body isn't on show as much, maintain moisturised, smooth skin. Indulge in home-made natural masks made from egg whites, avocado, and honey. Exfoliate dry heels, lavish with moisturiser and wear warm socks to bed. Continue to drink two litres of water a day. Evening events will continue throughout winter and you need to be at your glamorous best.

2. Surround yourself with warm textiles at home. Fluffy throws and cuddly cushions, perfect for snuggling inside.

3. Choose to stay home occasionally rather than doing the constant social whirl of nightclub openings, theatre and movie premieres. Curl up with a hot chocolate and stream the latest blockbuster.

4. Stay warm. Invest in a pair of snug fluffy socks and a cosy blanket to cover with while curled on the couch.

5. Scented candles are perfect for creating a winter ambiance. From vanilla to cinnamon, infuse your room with warmth.

6. Whip up a feast. Check out new cookbooks. Invest in a slow cooker. Surround yourself with fresh ingredients and herbs. And enjoy the results of your labour while whizzing around a warm kitchen.

7. Relax. Take a long, hot bath, slip into comfy clothes, pour a glass of red wine, and curl up on the couch with the latest best-seller.

Liza's WAG Wow tips

8. *Warm up. On rainy days, get active. Whether yoga at home or a local Zumba class, having a workout is good for the mind, body and soul.*

9. *Rug up and take a walk. Head to a local park or the beautiful Botanical Gardens near the city.*

10. *A rainy day is perfect for all those little jobs you've put off: sort through your old photos, spring clean your closet, organise your filing cabinet. You'll feel satisfied and warm by the end of it.*

11. *Pep up your wardrobe. Investing in a few key pieces will glam up your look. A good quality woollen coat and black flat-heeled knee-high boots can be used for many seasons.*

12. *Check out other sports. While WAGs get to attend all games of their partner, why not learn about a new sport? Melbourne is the home of Australian Rules Football in winter. Pick a team. Don the colours and show your patriotism.*

13. *If all else fails and the cold is getting you down, book a weekend away to escape and make sure it's somewhere tropical. Winters in Queensland are notoriously mild and after a two-hour plane trip you could be soaking up the sun.*

THE DAY SPA

For a WAG to have true wow potential at any event, a visit to a day spa beforehand is a must. Below is a list of treatments, from the basic to the sublime. Worth the time and money investment for body and soul.

Waxing
Eyelash tint
Spray tan
Mani & pedi (skip the basic and go deluxe)

Foot bath/reflexology
Body scrub
Clay body mask
Yoghurt body cocoon
Massage (including scalp)
Facial

If you're too busy to attend a day spa, set aside a few hours at home and DIY.

Cooled tea bags or cucumber slices work wonders to de-puff eyes.

Make your own moisturising face mask: Blend yoghurt, honey, avocado, and aloe vera gel, paint on face with a foundation brush, let it dry for 20 minutes and rinse. Refreshed skin!

Condition your hair with coconut oil. You can leave it in overnight for deeper moisturising.

Make your own exfoliating body scrub: 1 cup raw oats, 1 cup brown sugar, 1 cup olive oil. Mix together and apply on dry skin moving your hand in slow circles. Rinse off. Smooth skin!

Make your own hand cream: add a few drops of tea tree oil, lavender oil and olive oil to a few spoonfuls of cold cream. (For a fruity smell, add a banana.) Blend. Slather over hands, wear rubber gloves while watching TV. For better penetration, place gloved hands on a hot-water bottle.

THE HOME

While WAGs lead a busy social life, they do occasionally entertain at home. And even if they don't, what better way to unwind after a hectic game or a rowdy after-match function than kicking back in their cosy abode?

Here are a few tips to make your home entirely liveable:

Liza's WAG Wow tips

Make your entry foyer inviting.

When your guests enter your home it's the first area they see. The foyer should make a statement, give a hint of what's to come, and draw the guest into the rest of the house. Pictures on the wall are the easiest way to dress up your foyer. Same with floor coverings. Hall tables are a nice addition as you can dress them with signature or eclectic pieces.

Experiment with glass.

Glass instantly adds sparkle to a room. Experimenting with shapes and heights (e.g., vases, bowls, objects) is fun, and keeping them in the same colour palette is advisable. Varying shapes in like-coloured glass can be eye-catching.

Mix it up.

Every object in your home doesn't have to be an heirloom. If you like quality pieces, mix them up with a little kitsch. It's okay to have your favourite collection alongside that priceless vase. The whole point of collecting is to have a passion for it, finding items you really love, so why not show them off? They're a great conversation starter too.

Keep window dressings simple.

Whether you go for curtains or blinds, keep them simple. Don't let them overpower your furniture. Subdued tones work best but that doesn't mean you need to skimp on quality. The simpler the curtain, the better quality the fabric should be, like linen, silk, cotton or satin. Understated elegance is the key to setting off your room.

Layer your bed.

Your bed is usually the focal point of your bedroom and should be treated as such.

Layering different fabrics on and around the bed (from a fabric headboard to lush linens) creates an inviting room. When layering, avoid clash of texture and colour by keeping *it simple. Muted tones in green, blue and white work wonders.*

THE DREAM

For WAGs all around the world, New York City is the place to be.

From its iconic Manhattan skyline, to its most recognised Statue of Liberty, from the Chrysler Building to the famed Empire State Building, from its two most famous streets, Madison and Park Avenues, there is so much to tempt a WAG.

Throw in:
The Metropolitan Museum of Art (The Met)
Central Park
The Flatiron Building
The Guggenheim
The Brooklyn Bridge
Times Square
Rockefeller Centre
Broadway
Carnegie Hall
Lincoln Centre
Madison Square Garden
And it's little wonder that most WAGs dream of being a part of New York.
So what are you waiting for? Book that airline ticket now.

THE PROPOSAL

WAGs put up with a lot to stand by their man.
So it's only fitting a WAG deserves a special proposal.

Liza's WAG Wow tips

Guys, here are some of the best places in which to propose to your devoted WAG (and actually put that W-Wife-into WAG!)
Strolling along the Seine in Paris.
Atop the Eiffel Tower.
Cruising the Greek Islands on a private yacht.
Top of the London Eye.
Sunset on Legian Beach in Bali.
At the ball drop in Times Square, NYC, on New Year's Eve.
Winery dinner in the Yarra Valley, Victoria.
Hot-air balloon, anywhere.
Camel ride, United Arab Emirates
Walking the Great Wall of China
Outside the Taj Mahal
Climbing the Sydney Harbour Bridge
Cruising the South Pacific
Midnight on New Year's Eve, anywhere.
Central Park, any time
Spanish Steps, Rome.
Diamond Head, Waikiki
In a villa over the water, Tahiti or Maldives
Scuba diving in the Great Barrier Reef

THE BACHELORETTE PARTY

Once your sportsman has popped the question, it's time to move on to important things...like the bachelorette party!
Keep it classy.
Ditch the comedy genitalia paraphernalia.
Ditto strippers.
No nightclub tours via bus.
Have fun with your girls without the tackiness.

Liza's WAG Wow tips

Book a swank apartment in the heart of the city, order room service, expensive champagne and watch chick flicks.
A day spa package.
A weekend away in a posh B&B.
Eighties party
Hire out a renowned restaurant or use their private party room and indulge in fabulous food.
River cruise.
Cocktail party
Recommended cocktails:
Frozen daiquiris
Millionaire
Boomerang
Bossa Nova
Mimosa
Pina colada
Angel's Kiss
Avalanche
Chi-chi
Romantico
Pussy Cat
Margarita
Mojito
Golden Dream
Cosmopolitan
Jumping Jack
Flying Irishman

THE WEDDING

With a WAG's busy lifestyle, planning a wedding is a monumental task.

Liza's WAG Wow tips

For those with mega-famous sportsmen partners, the eyes of the world will be on you throughout your big day.

Here are a few tips to get you to the altar, smile intact:

Plan well ahead. Don't leave things to the last minute. And if it's too much, hire the best wedding planner in town and delegate.

Choose a theme for the wedding and stick to it. Makes co-ordination easier.

If intrusive crowds on your special day are going to be a problem, consider marrying overseas (eg. Bali, Fiji, Tahiti)

If paparazzi are a problem, sell exclusive rights to your wedding to one magazine and donate the proceeds to charity.

When it comes to bridesmaids and groomsmen, less is best. Keep it simple, classy, elegant.

Designer dress is essential.

Trial hair and makeup months before the big day.

Insist on tasting everything being served beforehand.

Funky cakes may look fun on paper but stick to the classics.

Madcap photos may appeal to the photographer but when it's your big day captured you might not find them all that funny.

Assign the rings on the day to the most responsible groomsman.

Fresh flowers.

Keep the guest list to close friends and relatives. Inviting the whole team may be your fiancé's priority but you don't want your wedding turning into an end-of-season trip rendition.

Make sure your playlist is loaded with all your favourite songs and plug your ears on the way to the ceremony.

Garter removal and bouquet throwing are yesterday.

Liza's WAG Wow tips

Prepare a classy speech. Why should your guy hog the limelight constantly?

Most importantly, make sure you book your wedding completely out of your partner's sport season, taking into account drawn grand finals, replays, and potential surgery due to injury.

Look fabulous, strut down the aisle, and embrace your WAG WOW!

FREE book and more

SIGN UP TO NICOLA'S NEWSLETTER for a free book!

Read Nicola's feel-good romance **DID NOT FINISH**

Or her gothic suspense novels **THE RETREAT** and **THE HAVEN**

(The gothic prequel **THE RESIDENCE** is free!)

Try the **CARTWRIGHT BROTHERS** duo

FASCINATION

PERFECTION

The **WORKPLACE LIAISONS** duo

THE BOSS

THE CEO

Try the **BASHFUL BRIDES** series

NOT THE MARRYING KIND
NOT THE ROMANTIC KIND
NOT THE DARING KIND
NOT THE DATING KIND

The **CREATIVE IN LOVE** series
THE GRUMPY GUY
THE SHY GUY
THE GOOD GUY

Try the **BOMBSHELLS** series
BEFORE (FREE!)
BRASH
BLUSH
BOLD
BAD
BOMBSHELLS BOXED SET

The **WORLD APART** series
WALKING THE LINE (FREE!)
CROSSING THE LINE
TOWING THE LINE
BLURRING THE LINE
WORLD APART BOXED SET

The **HOT ISLAND NIGHTS** duo
WICKED NIGHTS

WANTON NIGHTS

The **BOLLYWOOD BILLIONAIRES** series
FAKING IT
MAKING IT

The **LOOKING FOR LOVE** series
LUCKY LOVE
CRAZY LOVE

SAPPHIRES ARE A GUY'S BEST FRIEND
THE SECOND CHANCE GUY

Check out Nicola's website for a full list of her books.

And read her other romances as Nikki North.

'MILLIONAIRE IN THE CITY' series.
LUCKY
COCKY
CRAZY
FANCY
FLIRTY
FOLLY
MADLY

Check out the **ESCAPE WITH ME** series.
DATE ME
LOVE ME

DARE ME

TRUST ME

FORGIVE ME

Try the **LAW BREAKER** series

THE DEAL MAKER

THE CONTRACT BREAKER

About the Author

USA TODAY bestselling and multi-award winning author Nicola Marsh writes page-turning fiction to keep you up all night.
She's published 82 books and sold 8 million copies worldwide.
She currently writes contemporary romance and domestic suspense.
She's also a Waldenbooks, Bookscan, Amazon, iBooks and Barnes & Noble bestseller, a RBY (Romantic Book of the Year) and National Readers' Choice Award winner, and a multi-finalist for a number of awards including the Romantic Times Reviewers' Choice Award, HOLT Medallion, Booksellers' Best, Golden Quill, Laurel Wreath, and More than Magic.
A physiotherapist for thirteen years, she now adores writing full time, raising her two dashing young heroes, sharing fine food with family and friends, and her favorite, curling up with a good book!

Printed in Great Britain
by Amazon